KATHERINE GRANGER

HALFWAY TO HEAVEN

Published by Silhouette Books New York
America's Publisher of Contemporary Romance

SILHOUETTE BOOKS
300 East 42nd St., New York, N.Y. 10017

ISBN: 0-373-05536-6

First Silhouette Books printing December 1989

Printed in the U.S.A.

"You Look Utterly Delicious,"

Jed said, smiling. "So delicious, in fact, that I'm tempted to take you home and show you that a personal relationship with me would be infinitely more rewarding than a business one."

"What makes you think I'd even let you take me home?" Lindsey asked coolly, ignoring the goose bumps that broke out over her skin. She was so aware of him she felt dizzy, but she was determined to overcome these alarming symptoms and keep things strictly business. She had a second chance at getting the job, and she didn't want to blow it now.

Jed reached out and took her hand, turning it over to inspect the palm, then gently outlining each finger. "You'd let me take you home," he said in a low voice.

She dragged in an unsteady breath and tried to pull her hand away from his, but he insisted on holding it, tracing the thin blue veins at her wrist.

"Don't," she whispered. "Please, don't."

"You see?" he said softly. "You'd let me take you home."

Dear Reader:

Happy Holidays from all of us at Silhouette Books. And since it *is* the holiday season, we've planned an extra special month at Silhouette Desire. Think of it as our present to you, the readers.

To start with, we have December's *Man of the Month*, who comes in the tantalizing form of Tad Jackson in Ann Major's *Wilderness Child*. This book ties into the Children of Destiny series, but Tad's story also stands on its own. Believe me, Tad's a man you'd *love* to find under your Christmas tree.

And what would December be without a Christmas book? We have a terrific one—*Christmas Stranger* by Joan Hohl. After you've read it, I'm sure you'll understand why I say this is a truly timeless love story.

Next, don't miss book one of Celeste Hamilton's trilogy, Aunt Eugenia's Treasures. *The Diamond's Sparkle* is just the first of three priceless love stories. Look for *Ruby Fire* and *Hidden Pearl* in February and April of 1990.

Finally, some wonderful news: the *Man of the Month* will be continued through 1990! We just couldn't resist bringing you one more year of these stunning men. In the upcoming months you'll be seeing brand-new *Man of the Month* books by Elizabeth Lowell, Annette Broadrick and Diana Palmer—just to name a few. Barbara Boswell will make her Silhouette Desire debut with her man. I'll be keeping you updated....

Before I go, I want to wish all of our readers a very Happy Holiday. See you next year!

Lucia Macro
Senior Editor

Books by Katherine Granger

Silhouette Desire

Ruffled Feathers #392
Unwedded Bliss #410
He Loves Me, He Loves Me Not #428
A Match Made in Heaven #452
Halfway to Heaven #536

Silhouette Special Edition

No Right or Wrong #509

KATHERINE GRANGER

had never read a romance until 1975, when a friend dumped a grocery bag filled with them in her living room and suggested she might enjoy them. Hooked with the very first one, Ms. Granger became a closet romance writer three years later. When she isn't writing, she teaches creative writing and composition at a community college and freshman composition at her alma mater. Katherine lives in Connecticut with her cat, Barnaby. She enjoys movies, theater, golf, the Boston Red Sox, weekends at New England country inns and visits to Cape Cod.

One

For Lindsey Andrews, it was the worst day in the history of the world. Record heat and humidity blanketed Connecticut. Steam rose off the pavement in shimmering waves after an early-afternoon thunderstorm. Traffic jams on the interstates approached gridlock proportions as overheated cars stalled and irate drivers ranted at heavy construction that held up traffic for miles in all directions. The worst part was that Lindsey had a job interview at two o'clock. As she crept toward Hartford on Interstate 91, she kept glancing anxiously at her watch. She was going to be late, and to make matters worse, her car's air conditioning had unexpectedly broken down, leaving her suit a mass of wrinkles and frizzing her naturally curly hair into an uncontrollable mess. She felt like Curly in the Three Stooges. Or was it Moe?

She finally got off the highway, but it was impossible to locate a parking place. After cruising around Hartford for fifteen minutes, she got lucky and found a spot just vacated in the parking garage beneath the Wentworth Building.

Sighing with relief, she got out of the car, then groaned when she felt a tremendous run in her panty hose form an ugly ladder all the way up her left leg. Biting back a curse, she dashed for the elevator, only to catch her heel in the door. Horrified, she felt it snap off, leaving her with a three-inch heel on one shoe and none on the other.

"Of all days!" she cried, staring at the heel that seemed to symbolize what would probably happen in the upcoming interview. "Why this? Why now? Why *me*?"

She considered canceling the interview, then realized she couldn't. She would probably never get another chance. Fate had dealt her a lucky hand when Jed Wentworth had agreed to interview her for the position of publicity director. If he ever read her résumé again, he'd probably realize she wasn't qualified for the job and would relegate her résumé—and her—to the nearest trash bin.

Thus, limping like a lame duck in her wrinkled suit, with her hair frizzing wildly, Lindsey approached the august offices of Wentworth Enterprises. They lay protected from the world behind two-inch-thick glass doors on the top floor of Hartford's tallest building. Here, all was serene. Thick gray carpeting hushed all noise. Massive mahogany doors shut out all distractions. A secretary rushed soundlessly down the quiet corridor, a steno pad crushed to her meager bosom, eyeglasses perched precariously on a needle-thin nose.

Taking it all in, Lindsey felt her spirits dip. She didn't have a chance. She'd never be able to convince Jed Wentworth to hire her. It was rumored to be almost impossible to convince Jed Wentworth of anything, even on the best of days. He was one of Hartford's wealthiest men, a bachelor of legendary reputation, a civic leader, a phenomenon in the business world, famous for his wheeling and dealing and his flamboyant temper. A self-made man, he'd come from nowhere and turned himself into one of Hartford's leading citizens. He was said to be cantankerous, pigheaded, stubborn, and absolutely brilliant. If he liked you, you were a friend for life. If he didn't, you might as well leave Hartford altogether.

Summoning her courage, Lindsey approached the massive reception desk. Behind it sat an older woman with immaculate steel-gray hair and patrician features. Looking over the frames of her half glasses, she delicately cleared her throat as Lindsey hobbled toward her. "May I help you, Ms.?" she asked, somehow managing to convey the impression that a bedraggled woman with one heel was an everyday occurrence in this elegant environment.

"My name is Lindsey Andrews. I have an appointment with Mr. Wentworth."

"Ah, yes," the receptionist said, consulting a leather-bound appointment book. "A two o'clock appointment with Mr. Wentworth." She looked up disapprovingly. "You're late. Mr. Wentworth doesn't like that."

The words sounded ominous. Lindsey felt her heart sink but somehow managed to press on. "I know I'm late but I can explain why to Mr. Wentworth. Will he still see me?"

The woman picked up the phone and spoke in her low, cultured voice, then hung up. "You're in luck. He'll see you, but don't be surprised if he's less than polite. As I said before, he doesn't like to be kept waiting."

"Oh, thank you!" Lindsey said, backing away from the desk. "Thank you so much!"

"Don't thank me, Ms. Andrews," the receptionist said, smiling cooly. "Thank Mr. Wentworth. He's the one who's made the decision to see you." She gestured down the long corridor. "All the way to the end, then take a right. It's the last door on the left. His secretary is expecting you."

Lindsey limped down the deserted corridor, trying to wipe away the wrinkles in her once-pristine navy-blue suit. She hurriedly pulled out a mirror and inspected her face. At least her makeup hadn't run in the humidity. She tugged a comb through her wild mane of hair, then straightened her suit. Everything would have been all right if it weren't for the run in her stocking and the damn broken heel....

Raising her right foot on tiptoe, she practiced walking as if she had two heels, then gave up with a frustrated sigh. She could tiptoe when she arrived at Jed Wentworth's office. Right now, she'd just limp along and make the best of it. Then she heard a chuckle behind her, and stopped short.

Turning, her face flaming with color, she found herself facing the most incredibly handsome man she'd ever seen. He was over six feet tall, with broad shoulders, a muscular chest, flat stomach and lean hips. His dark hair was shaggy and unkempt, as if he'd brushed his hand through it distractedly all day. His blue eyes were twinkling, and one corner of his mouth was curled in amusement.

The fact that he found her amusing made Lindsey furious. Lifting her chin, she fixed him with cool green eyes. "It isn't funny," she said. "I have a job interview with Jed Wentworth and I'm already twenty minutes late and just look at me! My hair's a mess, my suit is ruined, and my heel caught in the elevator and broke off. *You* try showing up at an interview in a state like this and see how funny it is!"

Something flickered in his pale blue eyes, then he shrugged. "If I were you, I'd cancel. I hear Wentworth is a holy terror. I sure wouldn't want to show up looking like you do."

"Do you mean to say Jed Wentworth would judge a person on her looks rather than her ability?" Lindsey's eyes glittered dangerously. "Just let him try it," she threatened. She knew she was bluffing, but bluff and bluster were all she had right now.

The man chuckled softly. "What would you do? Punch him out?"

"I'd at least give him a piece of my mind," she said, bristling. "Now if you'll excuse me, I'm late as it is and you're just making me later."

"Good luck, Ms.—"

"Andrews," she said over her shoulder, hobbling gamely toward the last door on the left. "Lindsey Andrews."

At the door to Jed Wentworth's office, Lindsey stopped and took a deep breath to calm her nerves and cool her temper. She looked back in time to catch the man opening a door and disappearing from sight. Whoever he was, he set her teeth on edge. He reminded her a little of her old boyfriend, Ken Lawson, who'd set such high store on looks. Didn't ability count for anything? And what about gumption? It took plenty of it to show up at an interview with Jed Wentworth looking the way she did!

Squaring her shoulders, Lindsey opened the door and entered the plush outer office. An amazonlike secretary looked up, then simply stared, one iron-gray eyebrow rising in obvious disapproval of what she saw.

Lindsey began to feel as if she were trapped in some kind of Greek myth. Stumbling blocks were being thrown in her path right and left. If it wasn't unexpected construction on the interstate or a broken heel, it was an old harridan of a secretary who looked as if she ate nails for breakfast.

"You're Ms. Andrews, I take it," the woman said shortly. "Mr. Wentworth's expecting you." Her smile revealed what was clearly a sadistic personality. "I wouldn't be too confident about getting this job if I were you. I'm Margaret Oliver. I've worked for Mr. Wentworth for a long time and take my word for it—he detests people who are late for appointments."

That sounded like a death knell, but Lindsey ignored it. She went up on tiptoe on her right foot and lifted her chin defiantly. "Lead me to him."

Margaret Oliver stalked across the room and opened one of the double doors. "Mr. Wentworth? Ms. Andrews is here."

There was a contemptuous snort from the inner office. Margaret Oliver gave Lindsey an I-told-you-so look, then disappeared, closing the door and leaving Lindsey alone in the lion's den.

She squinted, trying to see in the gloom of the heavily curtained office. Staring at the massive desk, she realized the chair behind it was empty. As her eyes adjusted to the darkness, Lindsey looked around, noting the expensive leather couches and chairs, the granite slab that served as a conference table, the tasteful abstract paintings on the walls. Then a deep voice emerged from the shadows near the window, scaring the daylights out of her.

"You're late, Ms. Andrews," the irascible voice accused.

Lindsey's heart began to race and she hurried to explain. "Yes, I am. I'm sorry about that, Mr. Wentworth, but the traffic—"

"Traffic's no excuse, Ms. Andrews," the voice barked, cutting her off. "What would you do if you worked for me and we had a big presentation? Would you come running in late then?"

With only a voice to respond to, Lindsey felt as if she were shadowboxing. Ill at ease, she ventured toward the windows. "No, sir, I wouldn't. And you're absolutely right, Mr. Wentworth, traffic isn't a good excuse at all. If I worked for you, I'd be right on time."

"So what other excuse do you have?" the voice demanded.

"Well, parking in Hartford is horrendous," she said tentatively.

"So? You should have started out half an hour earlier."

"Yes, sir," she agreed. "I should have. You're absolutely right. Finding a parking spot isn't a viable excuse at all."

Suddenly a whirring noise broke the silence and the draperies began to open, revealing a tall male figure outlined against the light. Slowly he turned to face Lindsey. Just as she recognized him, he said softly, "Why didn't you use the excuse about your heel breaking off?"

She stared. It was the man from the hallway, the man she had detested. "*You're* Jed Wentworth?" she asked. It was her worst nightmare come true. She'd already met the man and made a fool of herself. From now on, she knew she'd spend most of her time just trying to bail herself out of hot water.

He walked slowly toward her. Her eyes were drawn to his brawny forearms. She watched in fascination as he rolled down first one sleeve, then the other. There was a strange pitching sensation in her stomach, making her feel as if she were on the prow of a small boat tossed about in unruly waters. Blinking, she raised her eyes from his arms and met his amused gaze.

"I suppose you think this is funny," she said in a strangled voice.

"I'm afraid I do," he said, smiling. "You have no idea how comical you look from behind when you walk. When I first saw you in the hall, I thought you were Chester, come back from *Gunsmoke*."

Feeling dazed, she stepped out of her shoes. "Okay," she said with quiet determination in her voice. "No more limp. Now can we get down to a serious interview?"

"You don't really expect me to take you seriously as a contender for this job, do you, Ms. Andrews?" he asked gently.

"Of *course* I expect you to take me seriously!" she cried. "I'm good at what I do!"

"And what is it you do, Ms. Andrews, besides make me laugh?"

She felt her world begin to crumble, but scrambled to make things right. "Look, Mr. Wentworth, I realize this interview has started with a bit of a handicap. Okay, a *huge* handicap, but if you'd just sit down and talk with me, you'll realize I'm a darned good publicist. I know public relations backward and forward. So far I haven't handled any projects as big as your plans for the plaza on the river, but I can do it, Mr. Wentworth. I know I can."

He glanced at his watch. "Okay, Ms. Andrews," he said, indicating a chair. "Sit down. Tell me a bit about yourself."

Letting out a thankful sigh, she sank into a deep, leather chair. He took a seat behind his desk and sat back, his hands laced behind his head. His body language communicated ease and power, but Lindsey refused to be daunted. This was her only chance and she meant to make it a good one.

"I have a B.S. in Business Management with a concentration in Advertising and Marketing—" she began, but he cut her off.

"Only a Bachelor's degree?" he asked idly, glancing at her résumé. "Most people realize they need at least an M.B.A. to get anywhere in business today."

Momentarily stymied, Lindsey cast about for an appropriate response. "Well, yes, sir, but my experience makes up for what I might lack in academic credentials. For example, my first job was with a major advertising company. I handled a number of commercial accounts there. Then I went to Peabody and Company as Assistant Director of Public Relations. I handled the campaign that changed our image from a small conservative company to a community leader. You've seen my résumé and writing samples, Mr.

Wentworth. You know I'm capable. Don't let a bad first impression spoil things."

"Okay," Jed Wentworth said, "I'll admit that you've done some nice things for Peabody, but they're small potatoes compared to me. This riverfront project is big. I'm planning a major hotel, a conference center, a condominium complex, an office tower, four restaurants, and a riverside marina. It will change the entire profile of Hartford. Do you really think you're capable of handling a project of that scale?"

"I know I am."

Jed Wentworth slowly unlaced his hands and lowered them to his desk top. "You sound very sure of yourself."

"I am, Mr. Wentworth."

"Why?"

"Because I know I'm good," she said, nervousness causing her voice to crack. She hurried on, hoping he hadn't noticed it. "I'm excited about what you're doing and I want to be in on it."

"Why?"

His quiet one-word question halted her. She stared at him, searching for an answer. She was in way over her head but knew the only way to survive was to swim like crazy. She began to talk quickly: "Hartford has an image problem, Mr. Wentworth. We both know that. When people think of Hartford they think of dull, conservative insurance companies and defense contractors, if they think of anything at all. We lack excitement.

"We're staid, Mr. Wentworth. We're not upscale and trendy, we're old money. We need to blend a little of the trendiness of Boston's Fanueil Hall area with some of New York's classy East Side. Your riverfront plaza will be the drawing card Hartford needs. The marina will change the entire river. With a skywalk attaching it to the rest of downtown, it'll be the best thing that's ever happened to Hartford."

"Your enthusiasm is contagious, Ms. Andrews."

Her spirits soared. She sat forward eagerly. "That's because I believe in what you're doing, Mr. Wentworth. I want to be a part of it. I want to be the Director of Publicity and Advertising for the Riverfront Development Project."

Jed pursed his lips and studied Lindsey, then shook his head. "You've got confidence and a lot of spirit, but you don't have the experience we need. I'm sorry, Ms. Andrews, but I don't think you're the person for this job."

Deflated, she sank back in the chair, then rallied. "You won't find anyone better."

"I think I will."

"Where?"

"New York," he said. "San Francisco. Chicago, maybe."

"But they won't have the feel for Hartford that I do," she protested. "They'll be strangers, bringing in foreign ideas."

"They'll be professionals," he asserted, "bringing in new ideas."

"Their ideas won't be any newer or better than mine."

"Ms. Andrews," Jed said gently. "I truly admire your spirit. I don't think I myself would have had the courage to show up for an interview looking the way you do. But courage and spirit aren't what I'm looking for."

"Well, maybe they should be!" She knew this was her last chance. Her back was to the wall and she was looking down the barrel of a mighty big gun. "Your riverfront project calls for both courage and spirit, and if you base your hiring decisions solely on what a person looks like, you're in deep trouble, Mr. Wentworth."

He looked at her for a moment, as if struck by what she'd said, then he shook his head. "Ms. Andrews," he said patiently, "public relations and advertising have a great deal to do with image, and if the image projected by the Director of Public Relations and Advertising isn't a cosmopolitan one..." He left his sentence dangling, the unspoken implication drifting like smoke in the air.

"I can be cosmopolitan!" she cried. "I defy anyone to look sophisticated and cosmopolitan if they lose a heel in an elevator!" She nodded decisively. "Even in New York, San Francisco, or Chicago."

The corners of his mouth twitched in amusement, but he shook his head. "I'm sorry, Ms. Andrews, but my mind is made up. You don't have the experience. Come back in five years. I'll be glad to talk to you then."

As if to signal the end of the interview, Jed Wentworth began to glance through some papers on his desk. Refusing to give up, Lindsey sat and stared at him. "It's not experience we're talking about here, is it?" she said slowly. "It's appearance. If I'd walked in wearing a fancy designer suit with flawless hair and both heels intact, you'd have sat up and noticed me all right, wouldn't you? You think I'm not sophisticated enough. That's it, isn't it?"

Appearing surprised she was still sitting there, Jed looked up. He studied her a moment, then steepled his fingers judiciously. "Perhaps sophistication is just another word for experience, Ms. Andrews," he said gently.

"You won't listen to me, will you?" she said tiredly. "You just won't let me convince you."

"I'm afraid not, Ms. Andrews." He glanced at his watch. "And I'm afraid I have another appointment."

Rising from the chair, Lindsey looked down at her bedraggled shoes. She was damned if she'd put them on and limp out, giving him another good chuckle. Picking them up, she tucked them under her arm and walked regally toward the door.

"You haven't heard the last of me, Mr. Wentworth," she said as she opened the door. "I'm convinced I'm the best person for this job, and until you hire someone, I'll be in there pitching to get it."

"Like I said, Ms. Andrews—I admire your spirit."

"Good," she bluffed. "You'd better get used to it. We'll be working together a good long time." She closed the door with a definite thud, then crumpled.

His secretary eyed her sourly. "I told you he wouldn't hire you."

The old witch's words put fire in Lindsey. She straightened her slumping backbone and put on her shoes. "He'll hire me," she said, her voice quivering but her determination unwavering.

Margaret Oliver arched a brow. She seemed about to say something sarcastic when the intercom came on and Jed Wentworth's voice crackled loudly in the air. "Margaret? What's on for tonight?"

"The annual dinner at the Businessman's Club at eight, Mr. Wentworth," Margaret Oliver responded, eyeing her calendar. "Cocktails at seven. Shall I reserve the limo?"

"Thanks, Margaret, but I'll probably drive myself."

Lindsey pretended to be struggling to put on her shoes, but she was thinking fast. Jed Wentworth would be at the Businessman's Club tonight. Somehow, she had to find a way to be there, too. . . .

Two

Lindsey examined her freshly coiffed hair and fingered the pearls at her throat. Against her slim-fitting black dress, they gave her the necessary class and sophistication. Or so she hoped. Tonight, her nylons were runless and her heels were glued securely to her shoes. Her shoulder-length hair was becomingly bouffant and curly, no longer the frizzy mass it had been earlier in the day.

As Assistant Director of Public Relations at the small firm of Peabody and Company, she had never attended the prestigious events at Hartford's exclusive Businessman's Club. Very few women did. But this afternoon she had wangled an invitation through a friend of a friend and now she handed it to the liveried butler standing in the door to the elegantly appointed ballroom.

The butler glanced at it, then smiled unctuously and bowed politely. "Ms. Andrews, how nice to see you this evening."

She smiled and swept past him, her head held high in defiance of the butterflies that had congregated in her stomach. She wasn't completely at ease in the rarefied atmosphere inhabited by Hartford's social elite, but she was determined to play the role. If she had been a mess this afternoon, she would be the picture of sophistication tonight. She'd show Jed Wentworth she could fit in with his peers and not make a fool of herself.

Taking a glass of champagne, Lindsey began mixing with the crowd. Luckily, she knew many of them and was greeted warmly, but as she chatted and nodded to acquaintances, her gaze continually swept the room, looking for Jed Wentworth. He was her goal tonight.

Sipping her champagne, she wandered through the crowded ballroom, laughing, smiling, noting even the smallest items of business gossip. It was networking at its most elegant, and she didn't downplay its importance.

Pausing on the perimeter of the room, Lindsey gazed around. This was what she was made for, what she had hungered for since childhood. She wanted to be a mover and a shaker, wanted to wield influence, to rub elbows with the rich and powerful.

But she also wanted something more, something she had tried desperately to communicate to Jed Wentworth that afternoon. She loved Hartford, had loved it since she was a child growing up in the west end. She'd watched it grow, had witnessed the spurt of development in the inner city, had gazed on, fascinated, as broken-down tenements were demolished, making way for new condominiums and trendy office buildings. In some way, however small, she wanted to be a part of Hartford's continued growth. She wanted to be in that magic inner circle that Jed Wentworth represented, the elite corps of individuals who had the power to change the course of Hartford's future.

For a moment, she pictured her father, frail and bent in his usual wrinkled suit, with a fraying shirt collar, his pale face perpetually lined with worry. He'd never even had the chance to enter the posh Businessman's Club. It had been out of his league. Remembering, Lindsey's face grew stony. He'd never had a chance to succeed at all. After working hard all his life, he'd ended up a shriveled failure, scorned by the world.

Lindsey's face grew colder as she spied Lyman Cartwright. She hated him with a passion. How typical that he would be here tonight. Only one thought comforted Lindsey as she stared at Cartwright with smoldering green eyes—she, the daughter of Henry Andrews, Cartwright's disgraced former business partner, was also here tonight. Somehow, that almost seemed like appropriate retribution. But it wasn't enough. Nothing could ever be enough. Lindsey's desire to put Lyman Cartwright in his place would never be assuaged until she herself had scaled the very same business heights he had conquered so long ago.

Resolutely, Lindsey pushed the disturbing thoughts away, determined not to let them ruin her night. Slipping into the crowd, she made her way toward the buffet table. Halfway there, she spied Jed Wentworth. He stood head and shoulders above the surrounding crowd, at ease and affable, so handsome he took her breath away. Lindsey paused, aware of a pleasant fluttering in the pit of her stomach.

She told herself it was merely exhilaration at seeing the object of her quest, but some honest part of her laughed at the lie. It was Jed Wentworth the man she was responding to, not the powerful magnate. At that insight, she stopped short and studied him more carefully. He was undeniably attractive, with laugh lines radiating from the corners of his blue eyes, a squared jaw, sculpted mouth, craggy brows and proud nose. He was truly arresting, the kind of man people stared at, taken in not only by his looks but also by his charisma. He exuded an aura of power, communicated leadership, symbolized everything the tough American male had come to mean.

But then, as if guided by sonar, his eyes swept the room and came to rest on hers. She felt that look from the top of her head to the tips of her toes, as if she'd been zapped by lightning. The rest of the room faded into a misty background. Only Jed Wentworth and she existed, alone in space and time.

She watched as he excused himself from his associates and moved through the crowd toward her. His mesmerizing eyes remained glued to hers, holding her captive. She couldn't have moved if she wanted to. She stood and waited, engulfed by a flurry of emotions she couldn't even name. She only knew she felt more alive now than she'd ever felt before. Jed Wentworth seemed to emit some sort of strange energy that permeated her entire being.

"Ms. Andrews," he said when he reached her, inclining his head politely. "It *is* Ms. Andrews, isn't it? The woman with the wild hair and one heel? How *are* your heels tonight?"

"Intact," she said dryly.

A slow smile crossed his face, beginning at his mouth and quickly reaching his eyes. "You look utterly charming. Is this for my benefit?"

"Why, no," she said, arching a surprised brow and gazing around, managing to look properly bored. "Why would I waste my time, Mr. Wentworth? You already made it clear what your decision was."

"But if I remember correctly, you made it clear you weren't buying my decision."

"So I did," she said, smiling. "But would that matter with a big wheeler-dealer like you?"

"No," he said, his eyes glittering with amusement. "It wouldn't."

Her smile faded. "Perhaps it's time you gave new, young blood a chance. You were young once, weren't you?" she added, deliberately catty.

He laughed out loud. "Touché, Ms. Andrews. I have to admit you have a certain way with words."

"That's why you should hire me as Publicity Director for your riverfront plaza project."

"You don't give up, do you?"

"Never. Not till the game's over, and as far as I'm concerned, it's just begun."

"Ms. Andrews, the game ended for you when I saw you limping down the corridor outside my office." His eyes swept her up and down. "Of course, that was before I saw you looking so ravishing tonight."

"Tell me, Mr. Wentworth, what would you do if faced with the prospect of choosing between two candidates for public relations director, one of whom had the best mind and brightest ideas but looked like a slob, and the other who dressed out of Brooks Brothers and Savile Row but couldn't come up with an ad campaign if his life depended on it?"

"Simple, Ms. Andrews—I'd keep looking."

"You're being slippery, Mr. Wentworth. I asked you a fair question. The least you could do is give me a fair answer."

"My answer was fair, Ms. Andrews. Now let's stop this petty quibbling and have dinner, shall we?"

He put his hand on her bare elbow and escorted Lindsey through the crowd. Her mouth went dry and her heart began to pound. Just the feel of his warm hand on her arm was enough to make her breathless and giddy. She wanted to escape his grasp, but somehow couldn't make herself. His touch was too exciting, too potently male. It had the exquisite power of making her feel fragile and feminine, of pushing business out of mind and propelling physical attraction front and center.

"Didn't you come with a guest, Mr. Wentworth?" she asked when she was able to trust her voice.

"No, Ms. Andrews. Didn't you?"

She glanced at him sardonically. She liked the way he kept her on her toes and just slightly off balance. It was like sparring with a heavyweight when she was only a welterweight. She knew he was playing with her, yet he was kind enough to let her think she was keeping up.

"Perhaps we should start over, Mr. Wentworth."

"Oh, don't be such a spoilsport," he said, smiling down at her. "I'm enjoying our relationship. It's rather invigorating, don't you think? I've always liked the idea of matching wits with a beautiful woman." His smile widened. "Of course, I like it even better when I win, and I definitely feel in a winning mood tonight."

"I wouldn't bet on it," she drawled, wondering where her courage came from. Maybe it was the champagne. Perhaps the bubbles held bravura.

"You see? That's what I like about you, Ms. Andrews. You refuse to be daunted. But let's not be adversaries right now. Let's put down our swords and enjoy our dinner."

They approached a table and he pulled out a chair for her. She took a seat, feeling a frisson of nervous tension ripple through her. She didn't think it would be a good idea to get too friendly with a man like Jed Wentworth. He was a notorious womanizer, and she wanted a job with him, not a broken heart.

"Does that mean we'll start being adversaries again after tonight?" she asked.

"That depends on what happens by the end of the night," he said lazily.

She shivered at the latent sexuality slumbering in his eyes. Suddenly she knew she was out of her depth. Her fingers trembled as she picked up her napkin and spread it on her lap. She was shaking so badly, she didn't trust herself to pick up her glass.

"Mr. Wentworth," she said, surprised at her own assertiveness, "I want a job with you, not a relationship." Since her aborted romance with real-estate developer Ken Lawson two years earlier, she'd given up on men and concentrated on her career. She wasn't about to let a devilishly handsome male do her in now.

"You're much more likely to have a relationship with me than a job, and let's stop this ridiculous last-name business. Call me Jed."

"Mr. Wentworth," she said with deliberate emphasis, "I mean it. I want only a business relationship with you. A personal relationship isn't in the cards."

"That depends on whose deck you use."

"We'll use mine, thank you," she said shortly.

"You see, Lindsey," Jed went on, ignoring her remark and causing her temper to soar, "what I find so fascinating about you is your spirit. Do you know how boring it is to be fawned over by every woman you meet? You, on the other hand, present a challenge. I like that, Lindsey. I like it very much."

"You can like it in the boardroom, but forget the bedroom."

His smile lit up his face, making him look extraordinarily attractive. Lindsey felt a shaft of awareness pass through her, heating her blood, making her skin feel frighteningly warm, as if it had been lit by a thousand glowing candles.

"Lindsey," he said, his voice low and intimate, "have dinner with me tomorrow evening. Not in a mausoleum like this, surrounded by a bunch of loud business types, but in an intimate little place where we can get to know each other better."

"I have no desire to get to know you better, Mr. Wentworth." She smiled to soften her words. "Except as a boss, of course."

"All right, then consider dinner tomorrow night as the second part of a job interview."

"Are you serious?" she asked. "Would you really give me a second chance?"

"Try me and find out."

She stared at him, hesitant, not knowing what to think. Then she shook her head, her spirits sagging. "No, Mr. Wentworth, that job means too much to me. I wouldn't want to do anything to jeopardize my chances."

"And having dinner with me would jeopardize your chances?"

"Wouldn't it?"

He looked away thoughtfully, then looked back at her. "Yes," he said, sighing, "I suppose it would. You're much too lovely. I'd have trouble keeping my mind on business if I were to take you to dinner."

"But I *will* take a second interview," she said, smiling. "How about Monday morning?"

"Monday morning's completely booked, I'm afraid."

"Then Monday afternoon."

"You are the most persistent woman!"

"Think of how that persistence would pay off in a public relations director, Mr. Wentworth. I'd bug the newspapers to do stories on our project. I'd keep our name in front of the public at all times."

"You know, Ms. Andrews, you almost convince me you could do it, but one thing worries me—bad publicity. Almost all new construction projects eventually run into adverse circumstances. Neighborhood groups organize to fight new construction, or somebody decides the project is going to hurt the community rather than help it and there you have it—one hell of a mess on your hands. With Peabody and

Company you haven't had to handle problems like that. I don't think you'd be up to handling them."

"Well, at least you're giving a sensible reason for doubting me," she said, "rather than just claiming I don't *look* right for the job."

"And I notice you haven't responded to it yet," he said gently.

She picked up her fork and toyed with the steak a waitress had set before her. "Mr. Wentworth, bad publicity is a public relations director's nightmare, but it's something that comes with the territory. I happen to believe in direct confrontation and honesty. I don't like sweeping things under the rug and pretending they don't exist. If a community group organized to protest the river-plaza project, I'd set up open meetings with them, allowing them to air their views, while giving us a chance to make our case. I'd want you to play a highly visible role. That would mean participating in the community meetings, not just cursing the rabble-rousers from behind those thick mahogany doors of yours."

"A refreshingly direct response, Ms. Andrews," Jed said. "I begin to think more and more of you as I get to know you better."

"Mr. Wentworth, I'm your person. Stop fighting it and give me a chance."

"All right, we'll set up another meeting for Monday at two. But this time, Ms. Andrews, come prepared. No heelless shoes and wrinkled suits. If you can look the part, you just might get it."

"There you go with looks again," she cried. "When are you ever going to realize that it's ability that counts, not appearances?"

"You're an idealist, Ms. Andrews," Jed said. "You're right theoretically, of course. It *is* ability that counts, but we live in a world where people are taken in by appearances. Very few recognize the real thing when they see it. So, Ms.

Andrews, a realist goes with the percentages, and I'm very much a realist."

"But tonight—surely you see that I can look the part, that I can project the proper image."

"You look utterly delicious," Jed said, smiling. "So delicious, in fact, that I'm tempted to take you home and show you that a personal relationship with me would be infinitely more rewarding than a business one."

"What makes you think I'd even let you take me home?" she asked coolly, ignoring the goose bumps that broke out over her skin. She was so aware of him she felt dizzy, but she was determined to overcome these alarming symptoms and keep things strictly business. Lindsey had a second chance at getting the job and she didn't want to blow it now.

Jed reached out and took her hand, turning it over to inspect the palm, then gently outlining each finger. "You'd let me take you home," he said in a low voice.

She dragged in an unsteady breath and tried to pull her hand away from his but he insisted on holding it, tracing the thin blue veins at her wrist that showed through the translucence of her skin.

"Don't," she whispered. "Please, don't."

"You see?" he said softly. "You'd let me take you home."

Speechless, she shook her head, her eyes wide and filled with fear. He was right. If he insisted, she wouldn't be able to resist him. He was powerfully magnetic and devastatingly handsome. The currents of attraction passed back and forth between them like electricity.

But she couldn't let him know that. She had to rein in her feelings and maintain control. A one-night stand with Jed Wentworth wasn't what she wanted. Slowly, acting with cool deliberation, she reached out her other hand and peeled his fingers from her wrist.

"I don't want you to touch me, Mr. Wentworth," she said quietly. "In the future, I'd appreciate it if you'd comply with my wishes."

Reluctant admiration glowed in his eyes. "You're good," he said, smiling slightly. "You're very good. Quite professional, in fact. It's nice to know that someone I'm considering hiring wouldn't let pleasure come before business."

His words hit her with the shock of ice water. Had he merely been testing her? Shaken, she looked away, trying to regain her composure. For a moment, she had almost yielded, had almost succumbed to the sensuality that had blazed in his eyes and burned in his touch. And if she had, she would have lost any chance at getting the job she so desperately wanted.

Gratitude swept through her on a rushing tide, but it was followed as quickly by a strange letdown. Something in her had wanted to believe he found her attractive as a woman. Now she realized he'd merely been testing her. For some reason, that hurt badly. Yet she knew she was being foolish. She'd passed his first test with flying colors. She should be celebrating!

Rallying, she cast him a cool glance. "I'm glad we understand each other, Mr. Wentworth. I want that job and nothing else."

He put his elbow on the table and leaned his chin in his hand, watching her as she nibbled at her dinner. "Such a shame," he said, sounding wistful. "I'll bet we could have made beautiful music together."

She rolled her eyes and took another bite of steak. "Hrrrmph. When I make music, Mr. Wentworth, I want it to be for considerably longer than just one night."

"Is that what you think I'm offering you? A one-night stand?"

"Isn't it?"

"Who knows? We'd have to see what developed."

"Mr. Wentworth, your reputation precedes you. You are a confirmed bachelor. I want no part of your shenanigans. Just give me that job and we'll make beautiful music together, but it will be strictly platonic."

"Boring," he said. "Utterly boring."

"You're really incorrigible, aren't you?"

"Mm-hm," he said, nodding, his chin still cradled in his hand. "In that sense, I'm a lot like you."

"Aren't you going to eat your dessert?" she asked, glancing at the luscious piece of devil's food cake on his plate.

"No. You want it?"

"Absolutely. It'd be a sin to let it go to waste."

"You have a healthy appetite, Ms. Andrews."

She cast him a knowing glance. "For food, Mr. Wentworth."

He smiled. "How did you know I was thinking of something besides food?"

"As I said before, your reputation precedes you."

"So you're not going to give me a chance at all, is that it?"

"Right. There's only one thing I want from you, and it isn't sex."

He sighed again and transferred his chin to his other hand, then sat watching her as she started on his piece of cake. "I like a woman who doesn't pick at her food," he said after a while.

She paused momentarily, her cake-filled fork halfway to her mouth. Was that a real compliment or a shrewd barb? She put her fork down and dabbed the corners of her mouth with her napkin. "I think I've had enough," she said, irritated that her voice suddenly sounded breathless.

"I don't believe it," he said, satisfied laughter filling his voice. "Can it actually be true? Has the ever-brave, ever-fearless Lindsey Andrews really had enough? Does this mean I've actually won?"

Lindsey's temper soared but she struggled to control it. If Jed Wentworth knew how much he set her off, he'd do it intentionally, just to spite her. He had the look of a rotten little kid who had once teased girls unmercifully. "Of course it doesn't mean you've won, Mr. Wentworth," she said smoothly. "It merely means I don't want to spoil my chances for that second interview."

He smiled slowly, his eyes thoughtful as he studied her. "You'll get that second chance, Ms. Andrews, but you'd better be prepared. If I should offer you a job Monday afternoon, be ready for considerably more than you bargained for if you accept."

Staring at him, she almost shivered in apprehension. What was he suggesting? Would he merely be a hard taskmaster, or was he saying that fending off his advances would be an integral part of the job . . . ?

Three

Lindsey tried to apply her mascara for the third time, but her hands were shaking so badly she had to stop. She was scared witless. Her interview on Friday had been a challenge. Seeing Jed Wentworth Friday night at the Businessman's Club had been a lark. But this interview today was serious, and she found herself so nervous she was tempted to call the whole thing off.

Her eyes wandered to the picture of her father on her dresser. Picking it up, she stared at it, feeling the familiar pain lance through her. With a sinking heart, she realized she was going on this interview for him as much as for herself. Long ago, she had vowed to fight his battle, and it had taken her to college on a full scholarship, then into the business world, where her father had failed so miserably. She could still hear her mother's strident voice, belittling her husband, nagging him, whining that he was a failure at everything.

"You're a loser, Henry Andrews!" her mother had shouted. "Why can't you be like other men? Harriet Simpson's husband is taking her on a cruise this winter. Think of it! A cruise!"

Cringing in remembrance, Lindsey saw her father's tired face, noted the weary slump of his shoulders. Even as a child she had wanted to shake him, to make him stand up to her mother and prove he could succeed, but she hadn't been able to. She did the only thing she could—she stood by him. Since her mother constantly ran him down, little Lindsey had to stick up for him. She did it staunchly, almost belligerently, hotly denying that her father was a failure. But now, looking at the photograph, she had to admit that her mother had been right.

Lindsey swallowed uncomfortably and put the photograph down, trying to push the thought from her mind as surely as she pushed the photograph away. She didn't want to think about it, didn't want to remember the painful years growing up when her mother ranted and raved and chided, and her father smiled meekly and nodded in agreement. Damn the man! Why couldn't he have fought his wife? Why had he let her bully him? Why had be been so disgustingly *weak*?

Lindsey pushed away from her dressing table, feeling sick from the memories, realizing suddenly she was more like her mother than she'd ever suspected. Eliza Andrews hadn't been weak. She'd schemed behind the scenes, trying to open doors for her husband, only to have him fail despite her best efforts. So one day she had packed her bags and walked out on him, inflicting the worst blow of his life, leaving him for his business partner, Lyman Cartwright. With Eliza's influence, Lyman prospered, where Henry hadn't been able to. Now, years later, Eliza and Lyman Cartwright lived in posh splendor in one of West Hartford's finest neighborhoods, while Henry Andrews rested, at peace at last, in a neatly tended grave.

Once, twenty years earlier, Henry Andrews had had a dream of turning the shore of the Connecticut River near Hartford into a showplace. He'd gone to every bank in Hartford for financial backing, and every one of them had laughed in his face. Now, twenty years later, Jed Wentworth was going to do what her father had only dreamed of. That's why Lindsey had to get this job. It meant everything to her.

Now it was Lindsey's turn. She'd grown up believing she had an almost holy mission—to succeed where her father had failed. She would make up for him, and in so doing, pay back her mother's treachery. She had worked hard in high school, had shone in college, then had begun the long struggle up the corporate ladder. Now she was nearing her goal but she was suddenly afraid. What if she were more like her father than she suspected? What if she too were weak? What if she, too, were destined to fail?

The questions left her anxious. She looked back at the photograph and her eyes filled with tears. Suddenly her heart swelled with compassion for herself and her misguided attempts to patch up the mess her parents had made. How sad it all was! Why couldn't they all have accepted what they were, instead of always wanting more?

Lindsey picked up the photograph and cradled it to her breast, giving it all the love, understanding and compassion she felt so strongly.

"Oh, Daddy," she whispered, tears shining in her eyes. "Daddy, I love you so much." Tears spilled over and ran down Lindsey's cheeks. "I'll do it for you, Daddy. No failures to disappoint you. Just success, all the success you ever wanted, Daddy."

She scrubbed her hands across her face and rubbed away the tears, determination glittering in her eyes. She wasn't going to repeat her father's mistakes. If it was the last thing she did, she wasn't going to fail. Nothing on earth would induce her to. *Nothing.*

Calmer now, icy with resolution, Lindsey began to reapply her mascara. It went on flawlessly. There were no smudges, no mistakes, no shaking fingers to bungle the job. When she finished, she sat back and stared at herself in the mirror. She shivered. What she saw there scared her a little. Right now, she would hate to be Jed Wentworth. Lindsey Andrews was on her way to the top, and nothing, not even Jed Wentworth, was going to stop her.

"You're on time, Miss Andrews," Margaret Oliver said dryly. "Perhaps you learned a valuable lesson last week."

Lindsey thought that Margaret Oliver was a bit too uppity for her own good, but she was determined to be polite to her. "I'm better than on time, Ms. Oliver," she said quietly. "I'm early."

She turned on an impeccable heel, displaying her flawless gray suit, her pristine white silk blouse, the expensive but understated gold necklace that circled her slender neck. Every hair was in place, every nail perfectly manicured, every hint of lint or a wrinkle banished from sight.

But though her outward appearance was poised, inwardly she was a wreck. Telling herself to think positively, to keep that stiff upper lip and be a winner, hadn't chased the butterflies away. She kept remembering her reaction to Jed on Friday night and wondered if she would grow giddy again at the first sight of him. Would she make the mistake of looking at him and seeing the man, not the businessman?

Worried by her thoughts, Lindsey sat up straighter, putting her heels neatly together and brushing a speck of imaginary lint from her skirt. She wouldn't think about Jed Wentworth on a personal level, she'd concentrate on the job.

That way she wouldn't sabotage herself by getting emotionally involved with him.

The buzzer on Margaret Oliver's intercom erupted and Lindsey jumped, then smoothed a hand over her skirt and pretended she'd only been restless. Margaret Oliver smiled knowingly as she nodded into the intercom.

"Yes, Mr. Wentworth, she's here. No, sir. Yes, sir. All right, sir."

Margaret hung up and went back to typing. Lindsey stared at her, then crossed her legs. One leg began pumping nervously. She realized it and caught herself. Putting both heels firmly on the floor, she picked up a magazine and flipped through it, then threw it down. She sighed and examined her nails, gazed at an abstract oil painting, inspected the rug.

It was no use. She was a nervous wreck. If Jed Wentworth didn't see her soon she'd jump out of her skin. She cleared her throat, hoping to catch Margaret Oliver's attention so she could make small talk, but Margaret went on typing as if Lindsey wasn't even there.

Lindsey found her dislike of Margaret Oliver beginning to surface. Margaret was an old battle-ax. Her hair was as gray as a cloudy January day. Her face was pinched and wrinkled, as if she never smiled. She seemed overly confident, pushy even, in a way that strangely irritated Lindsey. She didn't make any mistakes when she typed, either. But what really bothered her was that Margaret Oliver didn't tell her what was going on. She'd been here fifteen minutes already and she was still cooling her heels. If Jed Wentworth expected people to be on time, why wasn't he seeing her on time?

"Excuse me," Lindsey finally said, "but isn't Mr. Wentworth going to see me now?"

"He has an important phone call," Margaret said sharply. "He'll see you when he's ready."

Lindsey fidgeted in her chair. "Is it one of the applicants?"

"Is what one of the applicants?" Margaret snapped.

"That he's talking to?"

"Even if it was, would I tell you? I'm Mr. Wentworth's private secretary, not your personal conduit for privileged information."

Stricken, Lindsey looked contrite. "I'm sorry. It's just that I'm nervous and—" She broke off and looked miserably at Margaret. "I don't have a chance, do I?" she asked, all her high hopes dashed to the ground in one leaden lump. Suddenly she saw everything clearly. She'd been a fool to think that Jed Wentworth would ever consider her for the job of publicity director. "He's playing with me, isn't he?" she said, feeling more and more certain she was right. "It's a game. He's twisted. The man is sick."

"Ms. Andrews?" Jed Wentworth said gently from his doorway. "Are you quite finished?"

"Oh, Lord..." Red-faced, Lindsey turned to stare at Jed Wentworth, who had obviously been standing in his doorway long enough to hear everything she'd said. One brow was arched over gleaming blue eyes. One corner of his mouth was lifted in amusement. He seemed to be enjoying himself immensely at her expense.

She pulled herself together, picking up her briefcase and striding assertively across the reception room toward his office. "So the great Jed Wentworth has deigned to see me at last," she said, putting down her briefcase and ostentatiously glancing at her watch. "A full fifteen minutes *after* our agreed-upon appointment time." She smiled sardonically. "And this from the man who detests people who are late."

"Yes, but I reserve the option of being late for myself," Jed said easily. "It's one of the perks of being the boss."

"How convenient."

"Yes," he said, settling into his chair, "it is." He smiled and cordially indicated a chair. "Won't you sit down, Ms. Andrews?"

Feeling like a fool, she sat abruptly. Why had she let him get under her skin? She wasn't being appropriately professional, she was acting like a mare with a burr under her saddle.

"Well!" Jed said, leaning back and locking his fingers behind his head. "How are we today?"

"We're just fine," she said lightly.

He began to swivel back and forth in his chair. "Now if you'll just refresh my memory, why is it you're here, Ms. Andrews?"

Feeling like a kettle on simmer, Lindsey stared at him, her face growing progressively redder. In a strangled voice, she said, "I'm here for a job interview, Mr. Wentworth."

"Uh-*huh*," he said, frowning distractedly. "And which job was that?"

She glared at him, daggers dancing in her green eyes. "You know perfectly well what job, Mr. Wentworth," she said tightly.

"Humor me," he said, gesturing with his hand. "Refresh my memory."

She could barely speak she was so angry. When she did manage to speak, her words came out quivering with indignation. "The job as publicity director for your riverfront project."

"Oh, yes!" he said heartily. "The publicity-director job! I believe we did speak about that once last week, didn't we?"

She could have gladly strangled the man. He was pompous, arrogant, and hell-bent on humiliating her. He was a monster in expensive men's clothing. She hated him, but she was damned if she'd let him goad her into making a further fool of herself. Quietly, unobtrusively, she reached into her briefcase and took out a folder. "These are some ideas I came up with over the weekend," she said. She was chagrined to see her hands shaking as she passed the folder to Jed.

He flipped through it idly, then tossed it on his desk. "Interesting," he said noncommittally.

"How can you tell?" she asked coolly. "You barely looked at it."

"Executive prowess," he said, smiling slowly. "We business tycoons learn to judge things fairly quickly."

"Perhaps too quickly," she shot back.

He grinned. "Perhaps."

She tightened her fingers in her lap and tried to put a firm rein on her temper. "Well?" she asked, her voice slightly breathless despite her attempt to remain calm. "Don't you have any questions for me?"

"As a matter of fact, I do," he said. "What are you doing for dinner tonight?"

That was it. The final straw. She sat back in her seat, suddenly cool now that he had made it clear he was merely toying with her. "I've had it with you," she said. "You laugh at me, refuse to take me seriously, and then try to seduce me into the bargain. I've a good mind to—"

"Seduce you?" he asked innocently. "Whatever are you talking about?"

She stared at him, then rolled her eyes in disbelief. "You just invited me to *dinner*."

"So?" he asked, waiting.

She stared at him, nonplussed. "Well?" she finally asked, one hand held out as if in supplication. "What else am I supposed to think?" She nodded knowingly, her eyes filled with disillusionment. "I should have known you wouldn't give me a second chance. I should have *known* it! You've been letting me think you'd consider me for the job when all you're thinking about is how to get me into bed!"

"Ms. Andrews, I'm having dinner this evening with Clark Simpson, a local contractor. As a candidate for the job of publicity director for my new development project, you would be attending as a sort of third part of the interview process. Of course, if you're not interested, or if you prefer to think that my intentions are dishonorable..."

Mortified, Lindsey could only stare at him, flame-faced. "Oh, Lord," she said under her breath, "why am I such an idiot?"

"Do you always jump to conclusions, Ms. Andrews? Because if you do, there's little sense in coming to the dinner tonight. A publicity director needs a cool head, not a hot one."

She sank back in her chair, wishing it would change into an elevator and take her away from there. "I'm so sorry, Mr. Wentworth, it's just—" She raised her head and began to feel her confidence return. "You set me up, didn't you?" she asked slowly. "You let me cool my heels in the waiting room to get me irritated and then you mentioned dinner in such a way that I naturally thought you were coming on to me."

"Business is a game, Ms. Andrews," Jed said, steepling his fingers and hiding a slight smile behind them. "Are you sure you're up to playing in the big leagues?"

"If I had you for a teacher, I'd catch on soon enough," she said quietly.

He seemed to like her answer. He grinned and stretched, drawing her attention to his lean, muscular torso. She felt that familiar dip in her midsection and cursed him and his easy confidence. He was still playing with her. She felt like a puppet on a string—he moved and she reacted. Now he was making sure she noticed him as a woman notices a man.

Then he surprised her with a curve ball. "I'm wondering if you would catch on," he said at last. "There's something awfully naive about you, Ms. Andrews. One gets the feeling that you're a babe in the woods. I don't know, perhaps my first reaction was correct—maybe you should come back in five years, when you're not so wet behind the ears."

Feeling defeated, she rubbed her forehead wearily. "What do I have to do? I can't win with you, can I?" she said, staring at him bleakly. "You just won't take me seriously."

"But I am," he protested. "I asked you here today for a second interview, and I've asked you to accompany me to a business dinner. Now what will it be? Are you afraid you can't handle it?"

His soft question frightened her. She remembered her earlier fears, remembered her father and how he'd never been able to succeed at anything he attempted. Had she just sabotaged herself as surely as her father had done himself in, time and time again?

For a moment she wanted to get up and walk out, to leave Jed Wentworth and all he represented far behind. She didn't need his foolish games, his sarcasm and taunting. She didn't even need his job. There were rumors at Peabody and Company that she would be promoted soon, when old Peter Potter, Public Relations Director, finally retired.

"Well, Ms. Andrews?" Jed prompted softly.

She raised her eyes and stared at him and felt a hot coil slowly untwist inside her. "What time is the dinner, Mr. Wentworth?" she asked coolly.

He caught her gaze and held it, admiration in his eyes. "Eight. Shall I pick you up?"

"I can find my own way," she said.

"But I may want to talk business with you afterward."

"I imagine we could talk business far more effectively at the restaurant after Mr. Simpson leaves than at my place, Mr. Wentworth."

"But of course," he said, spreading his hands innocently as if he'd never meant anything else. "Did you think I'd try to go back to your apartment?"

"It crossed my mind," she said sardonically.

A slow grin spread over his face. "Perhaps you're not as naive as I thought you were."

"I'm glad you realize that, Mr. Wentworth."

"I said perhaps, Ms. Andrews."

She sat and took his measure for a full moment, then picked up her briefcase. "Which restaurant?"

"The Village Tavern."

"At eight?"

He nodded.

She nodded curtly in return. "I'll be there."

"On time, I hope."

"I'll be on time," she said coolly, looking back at him from the door. "Good day, Mr. Wentworth."

Four

Located in Avon, an affluent suburb west of Hartford, the Village Tavern wasn't exactly the type of restaurant Lindsey would have expected the debonair Jed Wentworth to frequent. It was typical New England colonial-style, with exposed beams, copper lanterns, a huge fieldstone fireplace, and pewter dishes lining the cherry-wood walls. Braided rugs covered the sagging, wideboard floors. A hand-stenciled sign in the lobby indicated that the Tavern had been built in 1825 by Ebenezer Elliot. Homey and quaint, it was known for its hearty, mouth-watering meals, rather than for its sophisticated ambiance or up-to-the-minute nouvelle-type cuisine.

When Lindsey spied Jed, her heart did a somersault. In his dark suit and white shirt, he was clearly the most handsome man in the restaurant. Staring at him, drinking him in, she could only wish he wasn't so attractive. Why couldn't he be fat and balding? Why didn't he chomp on smelly old cigars and slap people on the back while telling raucous dirty jokes? Why did he have to be everything in the world she'd ever dreamed of in a man? She cursed her luck and approached him, determined to be the complete professional. Tonight she wasn't a woman, she was a machine.

"You startle me," Lindsey said when she reached him. "I'd have expected L'Americain or even Hot Tomato, but never a colonial tavern."

"There's a lot about me you don't know," Jed said, smiling as he took her arm and escorted her to the cocktail lounge. "Stick around. Maybe you'll learn a few things that will surprise you."

"All you have to do is offer me that job," she said lightly, "and I'll be around all the time."

"Now why is that such an intriguing prospect?" he asked, his eyes sparkling devilishly as he held out her chair for her.

"You really are a rake, aren't you?" she asked as he settled into the chair opposite her. "That's such an old-fashioned word, but it suits you. Someday they'll stuff you and mount you in a museum right next to the dinosaurs. You're a dying breed, Mr. Wentworth—the Last of the Big-Time Womanizers."

"Surely you're not saying that other men haven't made passes at you on the job, Ms. Andrews! I can't be the only man who's seen beyond the business suit to the woman underneath."

"Other men realized a long time ago that a woman working alongside a man isn't a sex object. Other men have begun to see that a woman in business should be taken seriously, not treated as if she's dessert, after the meat and potatoes of business are done."

"So you *are* saying that I'm the first man to make a pass at you," he said dryly.

"So you do admit that you are making a pass," she countered just as dryly.

He laughed delightedly and ordered drinks, then sat back and studied her with amused eyes. "You intrigue me, Lindsey," he said at last. "You've obviously got the confidence to apply for a job that's far above what you can handle—"

"Far above—!" She stared at him, openmouthed, then snapped her mouth shut. "Go on," she said when the waitress had brought their drinks. "This is all terribly interesting."

"As I was saying, you've got confidence, yet I sense something else in you, too." He narrowed his eyes as he studied her. "Something vulnerable."

"Vulnerable!" She almost stumbled over the word, feeling her cheeks grow pink. "I don't know what you mean."

"You push too hard, Andrews," Jed said. "You lift that feisty little chin and dare the world to challenge you, but all the while I sense that you're shaking inside, not quite sure that you believe all the stuff you're spouting about yourself."

"Where's Mr. Simpson?" Lindsey asked, looking around nervously.

"He'll be here shortly," Jed said. "He called earlier to tell me he'd be a little late. Now, stop changing the subject. Let's get back to you. Tell me about yourself, Lindsey. Why do I get the feeling that getting this job is a life-or-death situation for you?"

"Do you get that feeling?" she asked, suddenly wary.

"Yes, I do. You're such a spunky little thing, but far back in your eyes, there's fear. Why? What are you afraid of?"

She fiddled with her cocktail napkin, not even realizing she was tearing it to shreds. "I'm not afraid of anything," she said, her voice quivering slightly. "What's there to be afraid of?"

"Lindsey," Jed said gently, taking her hand so she could no longer shred the napkin. "Come clean with me. Tell me about yourself. If you want me to hire you, you're going to have to tell me about your nightmares as well as your day-dreams.''

She looked away, wishing she were in Timbuktu, not Avon, Connecticut. Jed Wentworth was an even more difficult adversary than she'd first imagined. He read minds and saw into one's psyche. He was more than frightening, he was dangerous.

She cleared her throat and glanced at him. To her surprise, she saw that his face was filled with quiet compassion. That startled her. She hadn't expected to see compassion in Jed Wentworth's face—ruthlessness perhaps, and hunger for power and money, but certainly not compassion.

''All right,'' he said finally, his voice filled with gentle humor. ''If you don't want to open up, we'll leave it for now. But if you want to be considered as a serious candidate for this job, you've got to spill the beans sooner or later.''

''Spill what beans?''

''Lindsey,'' Jed said, sighing wearily. ''I know, for instance, that your mother is married to Lyman Cartwright.''

Twisting her hands in her lap, she said coolly, ''Who my mother is married to has nothing to do with my qualifications for this job.''

''I didn't say it did,'' Jed said. ''But I am interested in your background. I think it might account for why you want this job so much.''

''My personal life is off limits, in all ways. I won't date you, I won't settle for a one-night stand with you, and I certainly won't talk about my illustrious family history. I'm sorry if that offends you, but that's just the way it's going to have to be.''

''And I'm afraid that's not good enough. I understand about the personal involvement. You're a serious career woman and don't want to indulge in any shenanigans with the boss. I commend you for that. But I need to know more about Lindsey Andrews, the person. Sooner or later, you'll have to tell me more about yourself."

She lowered her eyes. "You're not going to hire me, are you?" she said at last. "This is your way of telling me I'm not going to get the job. You're being kind tonight by asking me to participate in this dinner, but tomorrow you'll find some excuse to let me down gently."

"I didn't say I wouldn't hire you. Right now you're still under consideration. How you handle tonight's dinner will have some bearing on my decision. How you handle some of my other questions will also determine how I make my decision. As of now, you're still in the running, Lindsey, so don't blow it because you're angry that I've read you like a proverbial book."

"Who's angry?" Lindsey asked sharply, her cheeks red.

"You are," Jed said, chuckling.

She wanted to deny it, but couldn't. "Maybe there is a reason I want this job so badly," she said carefully. "Maybe I'm just not willing to talk about it. But I can assure you, Mr. Wentworth, I *do* want this job. I'll work longer and harder than anyone else you could ever hire. Doesn't that mean anything to you?"

"Sure it means something to me! How d'you think I got to be where I am? Luck?" He shook his head and sipped his Scotch. "Uh-uh. Hard work, Lindsey, my dear. Hard work, a good brain, and leaving no stone unturned." His smile transformed his face and melted Lindsey's anger. "And a little luck, too, I'm happy to say."

"I don't understand you," Lindsey said, shaking her head.

"What's so hard to understand?"

"Your entire personality! On one hand you're demanding and ruthless and downright rude, and on the other..."

"Yes? On the other?"

"On the other hand, you're almost sympathetic. You seem..." She lifted confused eyes. "You seem almost kind."

"And that surprises you?"

"Yes, it does. To the best of my knowledge, nice men finish last—they don't become highly successful businessmen."

"Where'd you get your knowledge?" Jed asked wryly. "From the Marquis de Sade?"

Lindsey snorted. "Just read any of the current business bestsellers, Mr. Wentworth. They all tell you to take care of Number One first."

"And if you do that for very long, Ms. Andrews, you'll end up hated, envied and despised. No, simple human kindness is an old-fashioned virtue, perhaps, but it still has its uses."

Lindsey could only stare at Jed Wentworth. She had been raised in a household where her father had espoused human decency, yet had amounted to a colossal failure, whereas her mother had demanded push, drive and ambition and had ultimately left her husband for a more successful man. Who was right? Or was anyone right?

Only one thing was clear. Lindsey didn't want Jed Wentworth prying into her background. She wanted this job on her own merits, not because Jed Wentworth had the mistaken idea he owed her stepfather a favor. She despised Lyman Cartwright as much as she disliked her own mother and never wanted to be beholden to either of them for anything, least of all for the job that meant so much to her.

And for some reason, she didn't want Jed Wentworth to know about her father's own dreams for the Connecticut River. If Jed were an egotistical man, he might resent the idea that someone else had thought of it before him. He'd probably also resent Lindsey's presence on his staff, resent her ideas and suggestions. No, she had to be quiet about her background. She didn't want to do anything that might jeopardize her chances for this job.

Then she raised her eyes and looked at Jed and knew she was really in for it. Not only was she fighting for this job, she was also fighting her attraction to Jed. At any other time, she'd have thrown professionalism to the winds and let down her guard, but she couldn't now. This job meant too much to her.

Filled with dismay, Lindsey looked away. How was she going to keep her background a secret, remain the complete professional, and continue to resist the attraction she felt for Jed? It seemed an impossible mission. Sighing, she sipped her daiquiri and wondered if she'd bitten off more than she could possibly chew.

"Sighing so early in the evening?" Jed teased gently. "Is my company so abysmal?"

She cradled her chin in her hand and looked at him wryly. "Your company's outstanding. I'd give my eyeteeth to own even ten shares in it."

"You did that on purpose," Jed said, grinning.

"Of course," she said flippantly. "How else am I going to keep you at arm's length?"

"Then you admit it's difficult to want to keep me at arm's length?"

Stymied for just a moment, she bit her lip, then slid her gaze toward him, smiling slightly. "I admit nothing of the sort. Stop fishing for compliments. I imagine that ego of yours is very well nourished."

"And you're not willing to participate in its feeding?"

"Precisely. I'll leave that to all the deluded women in Hartford who think looks are all that matter."

"If looks don't matter, what does?"

"You see?" she said, laughing scornfully. "You couldn't possibly understand what a woman is looking for, Mr.

Wentworth. You're the prototypical male. You exude machismo the way animals exude musk."

"So enlighten me. What is this elusive something that women are looking for?"

"It's sure not what men want!"

"And what is it that men want?"

She laughed again. "One thing is certain—no man would ever put a woman first in his life. There're only two things on earth a man wants—money and power. Which amounts to one thing, really, since money equals power."

"For a twenty-eight-year-old, you certainly have a jaded view of men," Jed said. "Who says we wouldn't ever put a woman first? Don't you think a man ever wants cuddling and warmth and affection?"

"Oh, sure," Lindsey said dryly. "At the end of a long, satisfying day at work, maybe. After the little woman has cooked his meal and washed his dishes, after he's watched the football game on TV and tossed his dirty socks on the carpet, sure, he might turn to her for comfort. But don't try to tell me that's love, Mr. Wentworth. My definition of love goes a lot further than sex on a leather sofa."

"And what's wrong with sex on a leather sofa?"

"It's cold, for one thing," she quipped.

Jed sat back and cocked his head to one side, studying Lindsey with interest. "So, tell me about your definition of love. I'd like to hear more."

"I'll bet you would," she said softly. "Because I'll bet you don't know the first thing about it. It's foreign territory to men, Jed Wentworth. Love's an unknown country to the male species. You guys constantly mix up sex with love, and all you *really* want is someone to love *you*. None of you has the least idea what it means to love a woman."

"So, go on," Jed said, leaning forward. "This is fascinating."

"It's hopeless. I can't talk to you about love. Men and women speak two completely different emotional languages. A woman says the word 'love' and a man hears 'marriage.' He panics. He starts to envision little white houses with picket fences and baby carriages out front.

"He starts thinking Responsibility, with a capital *R*. He sees bills mounting to the ceiling and diapers in a pail and two o'clock feedings. Gone are his nights on the town with his buddies at the local tavern. Gone are the softball games and tennis tournaments and sunset sails on Long Island Sound. No more flirting with every skirt that comes along. No more juicy one-night stands with the newest redhead or blonde or brunette." She shook her head.

"Uh-uh. I couldn't even begin to talk about love with you. To a man, love is all about the loss of freedom. To a woman, it's about emotional fulfillment. We're on two different wavelengths on the subject. We might as well be from two different planets."

"You paint the bleakest picture I've ever heard," Jed said quietly. He picked up his glass of Scotch and squinted at it. "Maybe some men feel that way, but I don't think we all do, and I sure as hell know I don't." He put the glass down and faced her squarely, his eyes level and unflinching. "Know what I think, Miss Know-It-All? I think somewhere along the line you got hurt by a man and you've got one hell of a big chip on your shoulder. What do you think about that?"

"I think you're full of hot air," she said, but she had to look away from his too-knowing gaze. Memories of her aborted romance with Ken Lawson skittered through her mind, but she had no intention of discussing it now.

"Uh-uh," Jed said, shaking his head. "It won't wash, Lindsey. What was his name? Were you engaged or just in love with the guy?"

"He isn't important," she said sharply.

"So there was someone!" he crowed.

She gave him a dark look. She really didn't want to discuss her ill-fated love affair with Ken. "There was someone, but that was aeons ago. Believe me, I've forgotten about him totally."

"You may have forgotten about him, but you haven't forgotten what he did to you."

"He didn't *do* anything to me," she protested. "We just broke up, that's all, like a million other couples. It didn't work out."

"You loved him," he persisted.

She sighed. "I cared for him."

"Ah-ah, Ms. Andrews, the truth now. Tell the truth to Uncle Jed."

"You're *not* my uncle," she said coldly, "and you never will be."

"Well at least we agree on one thing."

She stared at him icily. Right now, she really didn't like him. He was too persistent, too sharp. But if this was the only way she could make Jed Wentworth think she was totally against men and marriage, she'd use it. He might finally get the hint and leave her alone. "Okay," she admitted. "I loved him."

"And you wanted to get married."

She flipped a hand as if it hadn't mattered. "Yes, I wanted to get married."

"And he bolted."

She almost smiled. Actually, she had been the one to end the affair, but she'd let Jed think it was the other way around. That way, maybe he'd get off her back. "Bolted would be the operative word," she agreed, smiling ironically. "Yes, the perfect word, in fact. He ran like a yearling in the fifth race at Santa Anita. He set a track record for escaping the clutches of a predatory woman, as a matter of fact."

"And you're still hurting."

"I'm not hurting in the least," she said, raising her eyebrows in protest. "I'm over the guy. He's old news."

"Okay, maybe he's old news, but the hurt isn't. That little speech about men and women and love had a little too much emotion in it for the hurt to be all gone."

She refused to answer. He was right, of course. Though she had ended the affair, she'd been badly hurt. But would she admit that to Jed Wentworth? Never. She sipped the last of her daiquiri and signaled the waitress for another.

"Lindsey," Jed said gently, "it's okay to hurt, you know. It happens to lots of people. It's nothing to be ashamed of."

She folded her arms and turned her head to the side. If she could have, she'd have blocked her ears so she wouldn't hear the tenderness in his voice. It might make her like him, and that could prove fatal to her plans. She had to keep Jed Wentworth at a distance. If she allowed him to get too close, she might not be able to resist him.

The waitress deposited another drink in front of Lindsey, then said to Jed, "Mr. Wentworth, a Mr. Clark Simpson called. He said to tell you he's sorry, but something's come up and he can't make dinner. He hopes you'll understand. He said he'll call you tomorrow to make other arrangements."

Lindsey unfolded her arms, picked up her drink and took a serious belt. "How convenient," she said when the waitress left. "I'll bet you had this little scenario all set up, didn't you? There wasn't going to be any Mr. Simpson at all, was there? Just a candlelit seduction scene, with little Lindsey falling panting into the tender, understanding arms of Jed Wentworth."

Jed dropped his chin into his hand. He stared at her, shaking his head. "I don't believe you," he said at last. "You are the most cynical woman I've ever met. Call Simpson. Ask him yourself. This was no setup. When are you going to start believing me?"

"As if I could!" she exclaimed. "I know about you, Jed! You're a dyed-in-the-wool, first-class, certified womanizer. You probably can't help it; it's probably in your genes, but one thing is certain—trusting you would be the biggest mistake I could ever make."

Something flickered in Jed's eyes momentarily, then he picked up his Scotch and sipped it, eyeing Lindsey over the rim of his glass. "If you can't trust me, then why are you so determined to get a job working for me?"

She hesitated. "I didn't say I couldn't trust you in a business relationship. You have a first-rate reputation as a businessman. It's your personal life that bothers me."

"My personal life? And what exactly do you know about my personal life?"

"Jed, be real," she said, exasperation shimmering in her voice. "Anyone who reads the business section of the *Courant* every Monday knows you take a different woman to every party you go to—and you go to a *lot* of parties!"

"So?" he said, shrugging. "Parties come with the territory. It's called networking, Ms. Andrews, or haven't you heard of that yet? I should think a competent P.R. person like yourself would be in on all the good socializing that goes on after hours. Surely you're aware that some of the biggest deals are cut across a dining-room table, not in the boardroom."

"I'm very aware of that, Mr. Wentworth," she said quietly, but she was thinking of her father. He had never rubbed elbows with the right people, preferring to remain home and read his precious books. She suddenly realized that her father had probably been in the wrong business. He hadn't been cut out to be a wheeler-dealer type. He'd probably have made a good absentminded professor, or perhaps a clergyman. He sure wasn't made of the stuff Jed Wentworth was. Or Lyman Cartwright, either, for that matter....

Five

In the middle of dinner, a waitress hurried over to Jed and Lindsey's table. "Mr. Wentworth, you have an emergency call. You can take it on the house phone."

Looking irritated, Jed apologized to Lindsey. "I'm sorry. This happens all the time. If the truth be told, it's the reason I'm still a bachelor. No woman in her right mind would put up with the constant interruptions. Sorry. I'll be back as soon as possible."

She waved away his apology. "No problem. Business is business."

"And business comes first, eh?"

She nodded, a slow smile curving her mouth. He was gone in an instant, striding powerfully through the tables toward the maître d's station. Lindsey followed him with her eyes, admiring him despite her attempts not to. Dinner was delicious, but the company was even better. Jed was humorous, polite, intelligent, and entertaining. For a successful man, he was amazingly modest, something she found enormously appealing. And though she had skillfully managed to evade all his questions about her background and childhood, he had drawn her out about her hobbies and interests. They were astonished to find they both liked science fiction, downhill skiing, and the New York Mets.

When he returned, he looked as if a storm cloud had settled over his head. His face was dark with anger. "I've got to go back to the office," he snapped. "Some fool messed up a contract and it needs to be redone and I have to sign it before it goes out tomorrow morning." He shook his head in irritation. "I ask you, why is it so hard to find good, reliable people? They're college graduates from good schools. You'd think that meant something, but it doesn't anymore. Good Lord Almighty, I didn't even *go* to college!"

"Well, I did," Lindsey said quietly, "and I can assure you, I'm as good and reliable as they come."

"Always pushing for that job, aren't you, Lindsey?"

"You bet," she said, grinning.

He relaxed a bit, breaking into a slight smile, then he tilted his head consideringly. "Tell you what—want another chance at proving yourself?"

"For the job?"

"What else?"

She passed on the opportunity to tell him what she thought he meant. "Of course I want another chance. When it comes to that job, I'll take as many chances as I can get."

"Okay, then come back to the office with me and proofread the damn thing. Lately I can't even rely on my word processors to type without making a mistake somewhere along the line."

"Proofread?" Lindsey said, wrinkling her nose disdainfully.

Jed sat back, a knowing look on his face. "So I found your soft spot—you think you're too good to do the small stuff. Don't want to dirty your hands with the peon's work, is that it?"

"No!" she said, sitting up indignantly.

"Caught you, didn't I?"

She bristled. "I'll go with you," she snapped. "I'll even type the damn thing if I have to."

"You just may," Jed said, grinning. "It's late and the word processors leave at ten. Know anything about computers?"

"I have one in my office," she said with a sniff. "And I've taken some courses at the local colleges. I'm up on twentieth-century hardware, if that's what you want to know."

"Okay, come down off your high horse and let's get going. Who knows how long this will take. If you want to work for me, Lindsey, there's one thing you'll have to remember—you have to be willing to do any job and work anytime. Does that bother you?"

"Do I look bothered?"

His eyes swept over her approvingly. "You look beautiful."

"Mr. Wentworth..." she warned.

He sighed and stood up, escorting her toward the door. "Okay by me."

Outside, Jed headed toward his car, his hand on Lindsey's arm. She slipped free as they passed her car. "Mr. Wentworth, I drove here on my own. I'd prefer to leave on my own also."

"Ah, that's right," he said. "I seem to remember that Lindsey Andrews has this notion I'm only interested in making a pass at her."

"Let's just say I'd feel more comfortable driving my own car to your offices."

Jed sighed and extended his hand to her car. "Go ahead, then—pass up the chance to drive in a fifty-thousand-dollar racing machine."

She looked at his high-powered foreign auto and shrugged with mock disdain. "My little car gets me where I'm going. Basic transportation, Mr. Wentworth—that's all a person really needs in life."

"You put me down every chance you get, don't you?" he asked, grinning good-naturedly.

"Just about," she agreed just as good-humoredly, then smiled widely. "See you at your offices."

She got into her car and drove off, absurdly happy that she drove out of the restaurant's parking lot before he did.

Midnight. Styrofoam coffee cups littered Jed's desk top. Papers were scattered all over the conference table. One lamp cast a cone of light on the pages he read at his desk, while another fell on the pages Lindsey proofread at the conference table.

Yawning, Lindsey rubbed her neck and stretched. Her back was breaking, her eyes were sore from entering the boring legalese on the unfamiliar word processor, and her head was reeling from the figures quoted in the document. If she had ever doubted that Jed Wentworth was Big Time, she didn't any longer. He dealt in budgets that rivaled the national debt, or so it seemed to her.

"Tired?" Jed asked from just behind her.

Startled, she jumped slightly. "I guess I can't pretend to be fresh as a daisy," she said, then twisted her head from side to side, trying to work out the kinks. "It's the back of my neck and shoulders," she said, shrugging and trying to remember the relaxation exercises from a yoga class she'd taken long ago. "That's where the tension gets me, every time."

"Here, let me help."

Before she could protest, Jed's warm hands were massaging her shoulders and easing the tension in the back of her neck. She went rigid, knowing this was unacceptable behavior on both their parts, but it felt so good she couldn't make a move to stop it.

"Relax, Lindsey," Jed said. "You're as stiff as a board. No wonder you're all tied up in knots."

She suppressed an ironic laugh. If only he knew why she was so stiff! It had nothing to do with the tedious and stressful work she'd just done. It had much more to do with Jed Wentworth and the skillful way he worked such magic with his hands. Against her will, she felt herself beginning to unwind. The muscles in her back and shoulders unknotted and her neck began to loosen up. She could feel the tension draining out of her, replaced by a delicious sense of languor.

"Feeling better?" Jed asked a while later.

She sighed wistfully and nodded, feeling as if she were submerged in warm, caressing water. Everything seemed to be moving in slow motion. "I feel absolutely terrific," she said drowsily. A contented smile curved her lips. She was as loose as a rag doll. "If you ever feel the need to change careers, Jed, you could make millions just giving massages."

"Right about now, I'd give a million just to have someone rub *my* back."

Before she could think, she said automatically, "I'll rub your back, free of charge." Then she heard what she'd said and flushed. Oh, Lord, talk about getting into hot water!

"You will? Lindsey, I'd be yours forever."

She turned and looked up at Jed and saw the tired lines in his face, the weary strain in his eyes, and she knew she couldn't back out. Pointing to a chair, she said, "Sit."

"No way. If I'm going to get a back rub, I'm getting the real thing." He made for the leather couch, whipped off the tie that had been dangling around his neck and unbuttoned his shirt. Lindsey's eyes widened as she realized he was going to take it off.

"Oh, you don't have to take off your shirt," she said quickly.

"Sure, I do," he said as he shrugged it off, looking as weary as a man who'd just run a marathon. Lindsey could only stare. There were men's bodies, and then there were *men's bodies*. Jed's fell squarely into the latter category. Outside of a fitness center, Lindsey hadn't seen a body like that except on the pages of the beefcake calendar hanging behind her bedroom door. Jed had muscles in all the right places, and they were the highly caressable kind. He was no muscle-man, bulging at the seams and looking like a sack of stones.

Instead, Jed was pure, primitive male. Black hair frosted his chest and trailed into a wiry V at his belt buckle. His shoulders were broad, his upper arms nicely developed, his back and midriff firm, without the paunchiness and excess weight that afflicted so many businessmen.

He turned and smiled at Lindsey. "Ready?"

She forced a bright smile and swallowed, then managed a cheery, "Sure!"

But inside she was trembling. The languor induced by Jed's massage remained, but was given a keen sensual edge by the proximity of such a desirable, half-naked man. She stared at him, lying so relaxed on the couch, and felt an unaccustomed eroticism flower inside her. She knew she was playing with fire, but she rationalized that she'd *promised* to give him that back rub. It wouldn't be fair to back out now.

Taking a tremulous breath, Lindsey inched onto the couch beside Jed and tentatively put a hand on his back. At the first touch, she almost flinched. He felt so good, warm and strong and his skin was as smooth as satin. She closed her eyes and breathed in his scent, then ran her hands lightly up his back, transported into some golden Eden. Palm trees swayed and the ocean whispered upon the shore and the music of violins soared amid bright fields of flowers....

"A little higher and a little more to the right."

Startled, she opened her eyes. She wasn't in heaven, even if it had felt that way for a few precious moments. Jed Wentworth was lying shirtless on the leather couch in his office and she was giving him a back rub. Rousing herself, she reasoned that she wasn't doing this for her pleasure, but rather for his. Suddenly that made everything seem all right.

"Ahhhh," Jed said. "That's it. That's just the spot. Perfect." He sighed contentedly. "Lord, that feels like heaven."

"It sure does," Lindsey had to agree.

"What'd you say?" Jed asked, his voice muffled because his face was pressed into his folded arms.

"Nothing," she said, savoring the texture of his skin as her hands moved over his broad, muscular back. "Just relax and enjoy it."

"I intend to," he said, and before she knew it, he had turned over and captured her hand in his.

Startled, she stared into his eyes. Maybe it was the hour. Maybe it was being alone with him. Maybe it was just insanity. Whatever the reason, she didn't stop him when he put a hand behind her head and drew her down to him.

His lips were gentle, yet provocative. They caressed hers softly, moving in slow exploration, not rushed or hurried or demanding. Without thinking, she responded, running a hand over his chest, relishing the questions his lips put to her. Her own responses were filled with trembling joy. A sweetness such as she had never experienced rose up inside her. She sank against him, surrounded by his warmth, inundated by his scent. How wonderful it was to hold him, to run her hands over his body, to feel his gentle lips kissing hers, seeking the response that seemed to come as naturally from her as water from a spring.

"Oh, Jed, you feel so wonderful," she breathed when the kisses ended. "I feel delicious, so—"

Suddenly, for no reason she could understand, she woke up. Sitting back, she stared down at him, stunned by the realization of what they'd been doing. Shaken, she put a trembling hand to her mouth. "Oh, good Lord," she whispered. "What are we doing?"

"Something wonderful," he murmured, his eyes warm with desire. "Come back. Don't go away now, not when we've just discovered each other."

He started to draw her into his arms again, but she stood up hurriedly and turned her back to him. She was trembling inside and out, petrified at the thought that she'd just succumbed to kissing the man she wanted to work for. Groaning, she closed her eyes and put her hands on the conference table, leaning over it, her head down, the picture of defeat.

"Lindsey?"

The sound of Jed's voice sent a terrible pain through her heart. The word around town about Jed Wentworth was right—he *was* a womanizer and a seducer. Given half a chance, he'd have had her in bed in ten minutes. Feeling sick at heart, she realized she had to salvage the situation. Straightening, she took a calming breath, and glanced at him. He was sitting up, pulling on his shirt, beginning to button it. She began to relax. At least he wasn't chasing her around the office, trying to get her back on the couch.

"I really have to be going now," she said brightly, pulling on her suit jacket and searching for her pocketbook. She wouldn't act the offended maiden. She would simply get out as gracefully as she could, chalk up her interlude with Jed Wentworth to experience, and not think about the job she'd just lost. That would come later, with plenty of tears and recriminations no doubt.

"Lindsey, I'd like to see you tomorrow."

She had to smile, but it was a knowing, cynical smile. Turning to him, she tilted her head consideringly. "Oh? And why is that, Mr. Wentworth?"

"You've interviewed for a position with my company. Or had you forgotten?"

"Have *I* forgotten?" Suddenly she could no longer play the sophisticate. She was angry, and Jed Wentworth was going to hear about it. "Isn't it more a case of *your* having forgotten? That little scene on the couch was what you had in mind all along, wasn't it? That intimate dinner in a charming restaurant was just calculated to loosen me up, then a sudden, late-night crisis filled with hard work to throw me off the track, and—bingo—in for the kill. Well, I'm sorry, Mr. Wentworth, but it didn't work. Not this time and not on this woman." Hurriedly she began to search for her car keys in her pocketbook, but her eyes were blurred with ridiculous tears and her fingers were shaking.

"Lindsey, I didn't plan this."

His words stopped her search. She blinked away her tears and slowly lifted her head. "Didn't you?" she asked quietly.

"No, I didn't," he said forcefully. "It just happened, I don't know how, but it did. It just seemed right. You must have felt it, too—"

She looked away from him, pain radiating in her breast. Yes, she'd felt it—the sweet beauty had filled her with an ache so wonderful she could have died and not minded, but one fact remained—it shouldn't have happened, and yet it had. And Jed Wentworth's reputation didn't leave much room for believing his hand-over-the-heart speech.

"Mr. Wentworth, let me remind you again—I applied for a job with you, not a personal relationship. Yet, if I remember correctly, a couple of nights ago at the Businessman's Club, you made no bones about what you wanted from me. But I wanted that job so badly I was bamboozled into believing you just might give it to me." She laughed cynically.

"Well, I was right about one thing—you did want to give it to me, but it was a snow job you were interested in. All you wanted was a chance to get me on that couch and see what developed. Well, you're good, Mr. Wentworth, but not *that* good." She was shaking now, but she didn't think it was from anger. It was more from a sharp, sudden desire to give in to tears and from the knowledge that she'd just been taken in by the smoothest operator in Connecticut.

As if he hadn't been listening, Jed ran his finger down his appointment book, then looked up and said impassively, "Two o'clock tomorrow afternoon?"

Startled, she stared at him. "What about it?"

"A follow-up appointment, Ms. Andrews, what else? This *was* an interview tonight, whether or not you want to believe it. What happened on that couch was completely unplanned. I may like my women, Ms. Andrews, but I'm not in the habit of mixing business with pleasure." He leaned forward, putting his knuckles on his desk and staring her straight in the eye. "All I can say in my defense is that I've just put in a nineteen-hour day, I'm dog-tired, and I'm a red-blooded male." He stared at her unblinkingly. "And now," he said, his quiet voice sounding almost dangerous, "What exactly can you say in *your* defense?"

Suddenly, not knowing how it had happened, she was on the defensive. Somehow he had neatly turned the tables on her and she was backed against a wall, her face aflame with embarrassment. "Well, I . . . I . . . I mean *we* . . . We just got carried away," she said, stumbling over her words. "I mean, it's late and we're alone here and we're both tired and—"

"Exactly, Ms. Andrews," Jed interrupted. From the grit in his voice, Lindsey knew exactly why he was who he was. Jed Wentworth might be a smooth operator but he was also as tough as nails, and right now he had all the force of a ton of concrete looming over her. "That's precisely what I've been trying to tell you. It *is* late and we *are* both tired." He sighed as if to demonstrate that weariness. "And let's face it, we're also human." He glanced at his watch, then straightened his broad shoulders and finished buttoning his shirt. "Now go home and get a good night's rest. I'll see you tomorrow at two for that follow-up appointment."

Staring at him, hope began to blossom within her. She didn't know how it had happened, but somehow getting the job remained a possibility. "You mean you'd still consider me?"

"There was never any question of my not considering you. Good night, Ms. Andrews."

She stood irresolute, not knowing what to say, then realized the least said the better. For some reason, tonight's debacle had been salvaged and she wasn't going to ruin things now. Lindsey backed toward the door, afraid to trust her luck. "Thank you, Mr. Wentworth."

"You're very welcome, Ms. Andrews. And thank you for your help tonight." He gestured toward the one-hundred-and-fifty page document neatly stacked on the conference table. "I couldn't have done it without you."

"I know," she said eagerly. "I really am the best person for that job, you know."

He looked up, his face dark with foreboding. "Don't push your luck, Ms. Andrews," he warned softly.

"No, sir," she said, opening the door quickly and hurrying out. "Thank you, Mr. Wentworth," she ventured, sticking her head around the door to peer at him hopefully.

"Good *night*, Ms. Andrews," he said curtly.

She gulped and slammed the door, then slumped against it. She'd won a reprieve. For the moment at least, she was still a candidate for the job she wanted more than anything. And she wasn't going to think about what had taken place on the couch. From this moment on, it had simply never happened, and that was that.

Lindsey pulled her pillow over her head to shut out the shrill ringing of the telephone. When it refused to stop, she muttered an oath and yanked the receiver off the hook. "What?" she demanded testily.

"My, my..." Her mother's cultured voice came floating through the receiver. "In a fine mood this morning, aren't we?"

Lindsey sighed and sank back among the pillows. "What is it, Mother? Want to sell me another ticket to a charity function?"

"No, I want to find out why you're home in bed at eleven in the morning and not at work. I called you there and they told me some cockeyed story about your taking a day off."

Memories of that same voice similarly chiding her father came flooding back to Lindsey. She shivered and closed her eyes, feeling like a child again, trapped in a home with a mother who was never pleased by anything her father or she did. They were never good enough—didn't work hard enough or long enough. Pain radiated through Lindsey. Just once, she wished her mother would tell her she'd done something well. Just once...

"I took a personal day, Mother," she finally said, her voice listless.

"What's wrong?" her mother asked sharply.

Was that concern in her mother's voice? Lindsey wondered, then shrugged away the ridiculous notion. "I'm exhausted, Mother. Don't worry, I haven't picked up any dread disease."

"I didn't think you had. You're just like me, Lindsey, healthy as a horse. But when does exhaustion give you the right to take a day off work?"

Cold anger simmered within Lindsey. What right did her mother, who'd never worked outside the home a day in her life, have to chide her for taking a day off? Lindsey bit back an angry retort and counted to ten. It wouldn't do any good to get in yet another fight with her mother. She never won anyway. When it came to fighting, her mother was a heavyweight champion.

"Lindsey?" Her mother's sharp voice recalled her to the conversation.

"Mother," she said tiredly, "I'm entitled to a day off once in a while. I work like a demon and haven't taken a vacation in two years."

"So what happened that made you take the day off today?"

"Nothing. I'm just tired, Mother."

"Nonsense," her mother said energetically. "Lyman told me he saw you at the Businessman's Club the other night with Jed Wentworth. He said you two looked awfully cozy. You're holding out on me, darling. What's the story? Is there a budding romance?" Lindsey heard her mother's quick intake of breath. "Is he there in bed with you? Is that why you're not telling me anything? Can't you talk now, dear?"

This time the anger that surged through Lindsey seared the blood that raced through her veins. She was unable to hold back the scathing remark that fought for expression. "No, Mother," she said coldly, "I'm alone. Unlike you, I don't choose to sleep my way to financial security."

There was an awkward silence, then her mother sighed. "You've never forgiven me for leaving your father, have you?"

"Mother, let's not start this again. You know how I feel. I haven't changed in ten years. Why should I change now?"

"You're a hard woman, Lindsey Andrews."

"You always said I was like you," Lindsey quipped with false cheer.

"Someday, Lindsey, when you grow up perhaps, we can have an honest discussion about what happened and maybe you'll begin to understand that I did the only thing I could do."

"Oh, I understand that, Mother," Lindsey said, pain vibrating in her voice. "Daddy couldn't make you rich and secure, so you found a man who could. I understand that perfectly."

"Lindsey, life is infinitely more complicated than you make it. Everything isn't black-and-white like you want it to be. There are all kinds of extenuating circumstances...."

"You're the Queen of Rationalization, Mother," Lindsey said sarcastically. "You could find a reason for killing someone that would make you look lily-white."

"All right," Eliza Cartwright said. "I can see it's no use talking with you right now. If you should ever find a forgiving bone in your body, Lindsey, give me a call."

Her mother banged the receiver down and Lindsey was left with the impression that she had been badly wounded by Lindsey's sarcastic accusations. Replacing her own receiver, Lindsey lay back and stared up at the ceiling, guilt pulling her apart.

She turned onto her side and curled into a ball, huddling under the covers while tears sparkled in her green eyes. Why was it always this way with her mother? Why couldn't she ever give her a chance? But how *could* she? Forgiving her mother would betray her father's memory, a betrayal even worse than her mother's desertion of him.

But some distant inkling seeped into Lindsey's perception—*would* forgiving her mother necessarily be a betrayal of her love for her father? Henry Andrews himself had always counseled forgiveness. He had been the most saintly, loving man Lindsey had ever known. When Eliza had left him, he had sat with Lindsey, holding her hand.

"Lindsey," he had said, "your mother did what she had to do. We weren't right for each other, you know. We never were."

"But she married you, Daddy!" Lindsey had protested. "For richer or poorer, in sickness or health, till death do us part. Don't those vows *mean* anything anymore?"

"Ah, Lindsey," her father had said, smiling sadly, "you're too much like me—idealistic, living in a fantasy world, where everyone is noble and all is fine. But life isn't like that, honey. Life is complicated." Then he had said something that still puzzled Lindsey to this day: "Vows made in ignorance should never be enforced."

"But, Daddy," she had said, her forehead wrinkled with confusion. "That's not true! Vows are vows! When we swear we will do something, we must always do it. Always!"

"My fine and noble Lindsey," he had said, rumpling her hair. "My beautiful daughter."

Pleasure at his praise flowered within her. "I won't desert you, Daddy," she had promised then. "*I* won't ever stop loving you. I'll love you forever. I swear it."

"Sweet Lindsey."

She had nestled her head against his chest and held him, vowing silently that she would never forgive her mother for what she had done. And so far, she hadn't.

Yet her father's words came back to haunt her now: *"Vows made in ignorance should never be enforced."* Something frightening stirred within her, some deep, primeval premonition that all wasn't as simple as she'd once thought. Her father had warned her of that, and now today, so had her mother. But if she gave in and abandoned her principles, she would be no better than a hypocrite.

Then she remembered what had happened last night with Jed. Suddenly, nothing seemed clear and simple. Confused, Lindsey glanced at the clock. In less than three hours, she would meet with Jed and find out if he would still consider her for the job. And if he did, would she dare to accept it? Last night, she had found out just how desirable a personal relationship with Jed would be. And for the first time, she was beginning to understand what might have motivated her mother....

Six

Lindsey sat in the reception room of Jed Wentworth's office, staring at Margaret Oliver, who was talking on the phone. But she didn't hear a word Margaret was saying. Instead, she was seeing herself with Jed last night, reexperiencing the sensations that had shaken her so badly. She was trembling, excited at the prospect of seeing him once more, but dreading it at the same time.

Then she sneezed for the hundredth time that day. It appeared she was coming down with a cold. When under stress, she always succumbed to the common cold. Soon her nose would be rose-red and her sinuses clogged. She would sound like a foghorn. She'd cough and sneeze and be utterly miserable—not that she could be any more miserable than she was right now.

Just as Jed's door opened, she sneezed again.

"Bless you, Ms. Andrews," he said. "Coming down with a cold?"

She glanced at him over the tissue as she blew her nose. "I'm afraid so, Mr. Wentworth," she said, her voice already beginning to sound nasal.

"Up too late last night, were we?" he asked, sounding disgustingly healthy and cheerful.

"I'm afraid we were," she said sweetly, then sneezed again as she walked past him into his office.

Jed closed the door behind her and leaned against it. "Then perhaps you haven't the stamina you'd need for the job."

Her heart dipped. She held a tissue to her nose and stared disconsolately at Jed. "Do I hear an ax falling?" she asked forlornly.

"Sit down, Lindsey. We have a lot to talk about." He crossed the room to sit behind his desk.

She slumped into a chair. "Just get to the point, Jed," she said tiredly. "I'm in no mood for sparring."

"All right, the point is—" he steepled his fingers and rested his elbows on the arms of his leather chair "—I still believe you're not ready to take on the responsibilities of Director of Advertising and Public Relations—"

Lindsey groaned and slid lower in her chair.

"—but I *am* impressed with your willingness to work and your desire for the job," Jed continued.

Lindsey hesitated a moment, then inched up higher in the chair. "And?" she said.

"And so I have a counteroffer."

"A counteroffer."

He inclined his head. "I'm going to need someone to act as a kind of liaison on this project, Lindsey, an assistant who can work with me and with the new publicity director."

"I see," she said, but she didn't. She sat very still and listened very intently. What in *heaven's* name was he talking about?

"I'm not talking about just another secretary," he said, as if he'd heard her silent question. "Margaret does a great job. I don't need a secretary. This is more like an administrative-assistant post, reporting directly to me, but with major responsibilities for the river-development project. I'm a busy man. I can't be spending hours with the publicity director, telling him how I want things to go. I'd leave that up to my assistant." He paused, swiveling slowly back and forth in his chair. "I'm considering you for that post. If you're interested, that is."

She was sitting up fully now, her back straight, shoulders squared. "I'm interested," she said slowly, "but I'm not too sure about the administrative-assistant title. That sounds as if I'd be going backward from my present job."

"All right, then how does 'Special Assistant to the President for the Connecticut River Development Project' sound?"

She ran the title through her mind, savoring it. "Special Assistant to the President," she mused out loud. "Not bad."

"Not good, either?" Jed asked.

"I'm just not clear on the responsibilities. You've been rather vague."

"Purposely," he replied. "The job is something I just dreamed up. It would be open-ended. You could make of it what you wanted. Write your own job description. It'd be your ball game, Lindsey."

"But I'd have no authority, no say on how things were done," she said.

"If you could convince me to do things your way, you would."

"That might set up a power struggle between the publicity director and me," she pointed out.

"I'm glad you recognize that," Jed said, smiling. "But then, by their very nature, all jobs are political and involve power plays. Are you telling me you're not up for that?"

"No, not at all. I'm just pointing out that it might happen."

"Don't you think you could handle it?"

"Of course I could!" she said, indignant. "As Assistant Public Relations Director at Peabody, I've learned how to get along with all sorts of people. It calls for diplomacy and tact, but I've managed so far. I don't have any reason to believe I can't manage now."

"Then you're saying you'll take the job?"

"No, at least not yet. Just who is your choice for publicity director?"

"I've offered the job to a man from Chicago by the name of Peter Gibson. He's quite good. I think you'll like him. I also think you'd work well with him." He smiled slightly. "I already know you work well with me."

At that she sneezed. "Don't," she protested, dragging another tissue from her pocketbook. "Don't even mention what happened last night."

"Who mentioned last night?" he asked innocently.

She blew her nose loudly, then stared at him miserably with red eyes. "I'm so embarrassed. I can't even understand why you'd offer me this new position after what happened last night."

"Perhaps I'm offering it because it was you who came to your senses first. You demonstrated a great deal of professionalism, Ms. Andrews, even when I didn't. That impressed me. Most women would have just let things happen, but not you." He cocked his head. "You know, some men might be offended that you prefer a job to a relationship."

"Personal relationships wither. Business relationships don't."

"There's still more than you're letting on, Lindsey, and one of these days, I'm going to get to the bottom of what makes Lindsey Andrews tick."

"No heart," she said ironically, tapping her breast. "There's only a Swiss watch mechanism in there, but it keeps perfect time."

"Good. That means I won't have to worry about your being late, like you were for our first appointment."

She smiled. "Never again, I promise." Then her smile faded. "One more thing. You haven't mentioned salary yet."

Jed laced his fingers behind his head and named a figure that made Lindsey's eyes light up. Her heartbeat quickened as she did a mental calculation and realized that her financial well-being would take a quantum leap if she took this job.

"Well," she said, sighing with satisfaction. "That's all I need to know. I'll take it."

"Great! When can you start?"

"I'll have to give three weeks' notice to Peabody," she said, "but I'll be happy to do any background work at night. Do you have any reading material I can go through to get me up to speed?"

"Glad you asked." He swiveled his chair and picked up a stack of papers about two feet high. "This will give you the information you'll need on the river-development project as it stands now. Read it over and get familiar with it. Don't neglect the legal stuff, even if it seems boring. I want you to know this project backward and forward. Think you can do it?"

"Piece of cake," she said, then sneezed.

"Right now, I think you need to go home and drink some tea and a dose of strong brandy. Sounds like you've got a nasty cold."

"I'll take these with me," she said, struggling to pick up the pile of papers.

"Don't bother," he said. "I'll have a courier bring them over to your place later. Go home and get some well-deserved rest."

She floated out of Jed's office, even momentarily forgetting her clogged nose.

Margaret Oliver looked her up and down. "I take it you took the job he offered you," she said sourly.

The vinegar in Margaret's voice brought Lindsey down to earth. "Well," she said defensively, "it may not be the publicity director's job, but it's still a good one."

"Didn't say it wasn't," Margaret Oliver snapped, then added grudgingly, "I don't know how you pulled it off, but for someone as young as you, it's a coup. You'll be working with Jed Wentworth himself. That'll give you opportunities no publicity director ever gets. You'll have his ear, every minute of the day."

Lindsey stared at Margaret, all the implications of her new job just beginning to sink in. "Every minute of the day?" she asked weakly.

Margaret nodded. "He's going to set up an office for you that connects with his. You'll be in his pocket. You'll go everywhere with him, attend all his meetings. It'll be the best experience of your life."

Lindsey smiled weakly as she left the office. It was going to be the best experience of her life—or the worst. For what could be worse than spending every moment of her day with the delicious but dangerous Jed Wentworth?

Lindsey's white-tiled bathroom was filled with steam. It billowed from the shower and hissed from the hot-water faucet in the sink, where Lindsey stood with a towel draped over her head, inhaling the hot steam in hopes of clearing her clogged sinuses. Stripping off her clothes, she stepped into the shower and soaped herself luxuriantly, enjoying the stinging spray on her aching muscles. Her nose and sinuses felt clear at last, though her hair was a mass of ringlets from all the humidity in the bathroom.

As she stepped from the shower, she heard the doorbell ring, and cursed. It was probably the paperboy collecting again. He always seemed to come at the most inconvenient times. She threw a huge terry-cloth towel around her and raced to the front door. Flinging it open, she came to a skidding stop.

It wasn't the paperboy. Jed Wentworth stood leaning against the doorjamb, a stack of file folders under one arm, his pale blue eyes appreciatively traveling down Lindsey's curvaceous figure. When he lifted his eyes, he smiled lopsidedly. Lindsey's heart leaped in her breast. Suddenly, the bath towel didn't seem all that big.

"What are you doing here?" she demanded, tugging on the towel to make sure she was covered.

"Enjoying the view."

"I suppose those are the papers you want me to read?" she asked. If she acted as if his presence were disturbing, he'd realize he'd got under her skin and that's the last thing she wanted. She'd simply treat him like any other male.

"Correct."

"You can put them there," she said, pointing to a small console table in the minuscule hall. When he put them on the table, she smiled uneasily. "Thank you for bringing them by. I appreciate it." When he didn't leave, she eyed him coolly. "Do you expect a tip for your services?" she asked.

"A cold drink might be nice." He ran a finger around his shirt collar. "It's hot as hell out there today."

"No air conditioning in your fifty-thousand-dollar racing machine?" she asked ironically.

"The car's air-conditioned," he said, "but walking from your parking lot to your front door was murder. The temperature's almost one hundred and the humidity's in the nineties."

"Don't step into my bathroom then," she countered, hitching up her towel and backing away down the hall. "I turned it into a steamroom to try to get rid of my cold. If you'll excuse me, I'll just go get dressed. You caught me as I got out of the shower. You'll find some beer and mixers in the refrigerator and there's liquor in the cabinet next to it."

"How is your cold?"

"Better."

He nodded, then again let his eyes drift slowly down her figure. "You'd better get dressed, Lindsey," he said softly when he raised his eyes. "We wouldn't want that cold to get worse."

"No," she agreed, her voice suddenly breathless. "We wouldn't want that." She was remembering the hard contours of his body and the silken feel of the hair on his muscled chest. Shivering at the vivid picture, she forced herself to turn away.

She dressed hurriedly, pulling on jeans and a T-shirt. When she returned to the kitchen, she found Jed seated at the small breakfast bar, sipping a beer as he stared out the window at the row of trees along the back of her property.

He glanced at her. "I guess I should have warned you I was coming."

"Yes," she said with light sarcasm. "It surprises me that you also act as courier for your own company. Or is that one of your cost-cutting measures?"

He smiled lazily and once again she had a quick but potent dose of his attractiveness. "Let's just say I wanted to get a look at the place where my new employee lives. It might give me some clues about what makes her tick."

"I told you that earlier today, Mr. Wentworth—what makes me tick is a Swiss-made watch."

"I don't think so, Lindsey. You wanted to work for me too badly. We discovered last night that it's not my body you're after, and presumably it's not my money. So, just what is it? Why is this riverfront development project so important to you? Are you really just an ambitious career woman out to climb the biggest corporate ladder you can find?"

"Would that be such a bad thing?" she asked, turning away from him. When he asked probing questions like that, she didn't want to face him. She had a hunch he was much too discerning and would spot any falsehood a mile away.

"Not necessarily bad," he said slowly, "if that's all it is. There's always the question of your past relationship with a certain rival of mine by the name of Ken Lawson. If it *is* in the past, that is...."

Stunned, Lindsey whirled to face Jed. "How did you—?"

"Lindsey, I may not be the smartest guy on earth, but I'm far from the dumbest. Our personnel department did its usual thorough background check on you before you even came for your first interview."

"Then if the check was so thorough," she said coolly, "you'll realize my relationship with Ken is very much in the past. We broke up over two years ago. As far as I know, he's dating at least three different women. We haven't even spoken in over a year."

"Then your desire to get a job with me isn't so much to help Ken as to get back at him, perhaps."

She shook her head. "I never even thought of it," she said tiredly. "Believe me, Ken Lawson is the farthest thing from my mind."

"So you want me to believe it's my fabulous reputation as a real-estate developer that drew you like a magnet, is that it?"

"No," she said baldly. "It's the particular piece of real estate you're developing. I told you the first day I met you,

Jed—I believe in what you're doing on the riverfront property, and I want to be a part of it. It's as simple as that. Take it or leave it."

"Why the riverfront project, Lindsey? Why that in particular? I'm also doing an industrial park in Avon and an office complex in Meriden, not to mention a rehab project in the west end."

She turned her head and looked out the window, remembering her father's dream. It floated in her head like a magic ship. "I think it's a wonderful idea," she said softly, then turned to him, her eyes filled with the heat of honest conviction. "More than anything, I want to see that project come alive. I want to be a part of it. I want to be in on changing Hartford's face. It's a dream I've had for years. You just happened to be the man who put it into action."

"So even if the man were Ken Lawson, you'd still want to work on the project?"

Lindsey laughed. "Believe me, Ken Lawson would never think of developing the riverfront. He has all the vision of a bat at midday."

Jed grinned and took a swig of his beer. "You just convinced me it's over between you and Ken, more than you could have if you'd sworn on a stack of bibles." He set the bottle down, then glanced up at Lindsey. "But you've also left some doubt in my mind."

"Doubt?" She frowned. "About what?"

"Your lack of admiration for Lawson makes it obvious just how much you admire me." His eyes flickered down her figure, then up again. "And the way you looked at me when you opened the door didn't leave much to the imagination, either. So I'm beginning to doubt what you've said about not wanting a personal relationship. I listen with my head, Lindsey, but my heart's telling me what I'm hearing doesn't ring true."

Hot color flooded Lindsey's face. "Of all the colossal egos," she said, "yours takes the cake. You just can't stand it that I'm not falling into your arms and begging you to make love to me!"

"Lindsey, let's get one thing straight, okay? We're working together now and I'll be happy to abide by your wishes that we don't get involved. But one thing I won't tolerate is lying. If you choose not to act on your desires, that's one thing, but if you try to lie to me, that's another thing entirely. I expect complete and utter honesty from my employees, Lindsey. I'm the boss now, remember? If you haven't given your notice at Peabody yet, you might want to reconsider. Think about it overnight. Think about it long and hard. But most of all, stop fooling yourself, because you're not fooling me at all."

She felt as if she'd been slapped, but refused to show it. Inching backward, she kept a tight rein on her emotions. "I'm not trying to fool anyone, Mr. Wentworth," she said in a voice that trembled slightly. "I'm just interested in doing the best job I can. I don't want to jeopardize it by getting involved with you. Maybe that's hard for you to believe, given your history with the ladies, but that's the way it is. I'm sorry if that wounds your ego but I'm sure you'll recover."

Jed narrowed his eyes and studied her, then casually set the beer bottle on the counter and walked toward the front door. "You almost make me want to prove you a liar."

"You couldn't if you tried," she said coldly.

"Don't tempt me, Lindsey," he said, smiling lazily. "Push a little too far and you just might find yourself in a very interesting corner."

He opened the door and was gone, leaving Lindsey alone and shaken. Leaning against the kitchen counter, she crossed her arms over her breasts and willed her heart to stop beating like a drum. Half an hour later, she was still agitated, but she'd made up her mind. Nothing was going to prevent her from taking that job, not Jed Wentworth or the devil himself. Come to think of it, Jed Wentworth just might *be* the devil himself...!

Seven

Lindsey spent her last three weeks at Peabody and Company clearing up minor projects and leaving notes for the next assistant public relations director. She neither saw nor spoke to Jed Wentworth, which promoted a sense of confidence and well-being. Jed lost some of his larger-than-life qualities and became just another man, someone Lindsey had once found attractive but who was now strictly off limits. He was going to be her boss, and that effectively put the kibosh on a personal relationship with him.

At night, she nestled comfortably in her bed and read the stack of papers that Jed had brought over. Most were boring legal documents, over which her head nodded and her eyes closed. Some, such as the initial architectural renderings, were absolutely intriguing. She would hold the renderings in her lap and gaze into the future with fascination, seeing the buildings rise slowly in her mind's eye. Soon they soared in her imagination, towering above Hartford's skyline, reflected in the rippling waters of the Connecticut River. They were magic buildings, floating in her consciousness like gilded rafts on an oriental river, shimmering in the sunlight, glowing in the moonlight. They seemed to come to life, became breathing Goliaths, redolent of cedar and freshly poured concrete, of sawdust and welded steel.

At those moments, her pulse quickened and she thought of her father, remembering his failed dream of developing the riverfront.

"We're going to do it, Daddy!" she said out loud one night, her eyes shining, her heartbeat thudding with anticipation. "We're going to *do* it!"

She hugged the architect's drawings to her breast and blinked back tears of joy. If only her father were alive today! How proud he'd be that his idea had taken root and was flourishing. She could see him now, his thin, gray hair blowing in the stiff breeze off the river, staring at the culmination of all his dreams.

"Oh, Daddy," she whispered, tears glittering in her eyes. "Your idea will live forever, I promise you. No shoddy buildings or poorly designed space. You'll be proud of it all, Daddy, I swear you will."

When the phone rang, Lindsey jumped, suddenly embarrassed that she'd been caught talking out loud to ghosts. "Hello?" she answered.

"Lindsey!" said her mother vivaciously, "What's this I hear about your going to work for Jed Wentworth?"

Lindsey's heart fell. She brushed away the errant teardrops and settled back against her headboard. "It's true, Mother. Your grapevine remains unrivaled in Hartford."

"So *that's* what that dinner at the Businessman's Club was all about—it wasn't romance at all."

Did her mother sound slightly disappointed? "That's right, Mother. Sorry, but there's no whiff of scandal here. I leave that to you. You're such an expert at it."

Her mother sighed. "Lindsey, won't you ever let me forget that episode? It was ten years ago. For heaven's sake, dear, let bygones be bygones. I miss you, darling. I want to make peace."

"You should have thought of that ten years ago," Lindsey said woodenly, staring across the room at the black-and-white photograph of her father. She needed to look at it to keep up her strength; otherwise she might be tempted to forgive her mother, and she couldn't do that.

"Oh, Lindsey," Eliza Cartwright said sadly, "I wish you'd stop this foolishness. I know you loved your father and I know I hurt you badly when I left him, but can't you even consider my point of view?"

"I did consider it, Mother!" Lindsey cried. "You were miserably unhappy with Daddy and you saw your chance at the golden ring and you took it. You bailed out. You left Daddy to his drinking and his broken dreams and you got that big beautiful house in West Hartford and the shiny cars and the cleaning lady and the caterers for your splashy parties and the pretty new dresses. Oh, don't think I haven't thought about your point of view, Mother. I've thought about little else for the past ten years."

"You're right about one thing, Lindsey," her mother said with quiet dignity. "I was miserably unhappy with your father."

Chastened, Lindsey nibbled on her lower lip. Something about her mother's tone of voice reached her, made her doubt her long-held beliefs. Maybe there was more to it than Lindsey knew. Maybe she should give her mother a chance to explain.

Then Lindsey rallied. Nonsense! Her mother had had ten years to explain and hadn't bothered. Why was she trying now? Because Lindsey was suddenly working for Jed Wentworth? Lindsey's eyes narrowed as she suspected she'd stumbled on the truth—now that Lindsey was connected with the wealthiest, most successful man in Hartford, Eliza Cartwright wanted to make peace. How touching.

"I'm sorry, Mother," Lindsey said, "but I really don't want to talk about this any longer."

"Well, we're going to have to talk about it someday," Eliza said, ever practical.

"Why?" Lindsey demanded. "You haven't seen fit to talk about it these past ten years."

"Why?" Eliza echoed sadly. "I'll tell you why—I looked in the mirror a few weeks ago and realized I'm getting old. I need my daughter. I need grandchildren. You're all I've got."

Again, Lindsey felt a pang at her mother's obvious sincerity. There was nothing phony about her words or how she said them. What had seemed so simple these past ten years suddenly seemed enormously complicated, and she didn't feel ready to deal with it. She reiterated her question, but this time her voice choked on it. "Why didn't you think of all this ten years ago, Mother?"

"I did!" her mother cried. "I thought and thought about it, but every time I figured you'd forgive me someday and come around. Only you haven't. You're just like me, Lindsey—stubborn."

Lindsey eyed the discarded architectural drawings sadly. "You know, Mother, I've always thought that if you'd put half the energy *behind* Daddy that you put into constantly belittling him, he'd have succeeded, just the way Lyman Cartwright did."

"Sweetheart, I *did* believe in your father when we first married. He was filled with such dreams, Lindsey, such fine and wonderful dreams. But little by little, as the years went by, the dreams never materialized and I began to realize I'd married a dreamer, not a doer, and I saw I wasn't right for your father. He needed someone softer, someone with less ambition than me. I admit it—I'm a pushy woman, a strong woman. I'm afraid I was *too* strong for Henry. I overpowered him. Finally I realized that I wasn't helping him, I was actually hurting him by staying with him. When I met Lyman, I saw in him everything I'd once thought I saw in your father. I fell in love with Lyman, Lindsey. Can't you understand that, at least?"

Falling in love? Lindsey immediately thought of Jed Wentworth and felt a curious pang near her heart. But she wasn't falling in love with Jed—she was just attracted to him.

"I don't know, Mother," Lindsey said. "Right now I don't understand anything very well. I'm confused. Give me some time to sort things out."

"I'll give you all the time you need," her mother said, her voice filled with optimism. "Oh, Lindsey, I do hope you'll begin to understand and forgive me. I love you, darling, and I miss you terribly."

Lindsey started to swallow, but there seemed to be a lump lodged in her throat. She couldn't even speak. Unwanted tears filled her eyes, making her feel frightened and vulnerable. Something wasn't right here. This was the way she always felt about her *father*. She'd never felt this way about her mother, at least not for years. . . .

"Mother, I have to go," she said quickly, forcing out the words despite the fact that she sounded half-strangled.

"Yes, yes, of course, dear," her mother said happily. "I'll talk to you soon."

"Yes," Lindsey said woodenly, then slammed down the receiver and burst into tears.

She cried until she thought her heart would break. She realized belatedly just how much she had always needed her mother. But somehow she'd convinced herself she didn't. She had erected a wall against her mother, making her everything bad and evil, while her father became the White Knight, all good and fine and noble.

What a fool she'd been! Pretending all these years that she needed no one, when in fact she needed her mother desperately, especially since her father's death eight years ago. Until she'd heard her mother's declaration of love, Lindsey's heart had been stone. Suddenly the stone was shattered and pain pierced her breast. She saw her stupidity, her stubbornness, her cold indifference to her mother's pleas for understanding. She saw it all and there was no escaping the self-knowledge and the accompanying pain that brought.

Yet pride still reigned. She couldn't call her mother now and tell her what she'd discovered with such shocking suddenness. Ten years of behavior couldn't be changed overnight. She needed time to sort it all out, to rethink everything that had once seemed so obvious, but was now so disturbingly unclear.

Lindsey looked down at the discarded architectural drawings. With these new discoveries about her mother, more questions arose. Why did she really want this job with Jed? For the first time, she questioned her real motives. Was she really just trying to make a name for herself? Was she trying to bring her father's dreams to fruition at last? Or was she merely getting back at her mother, repaying her mother's abandonment of her and her father by showing Eliza that her daughter could be successful in her own right, something Eliza Cartwright hadn't been able to do?

But there was another possibility also, one that Jed Wentworth favored—that she didn't really want the *job* with Jed at all. What she really wanted was Jed himself.

Thoughtfully, Lindsey stared into space, wondering how she could even begin to judge her mother when she didn't know the least thing about her own motives.

The first day on the job at Wentworth Enterprises, Lindsey stood in the main lobby of the skyscraper and watched as hordes of people scurried toward the banks of waiting elevators that would whisk them to the myriad businesses housed in the forty-five-story building. Wentworth Enterprises occupied the top four floors.

Lindsey approached the penthouse-level elevator with unusual caution. She didn't want her heel to snap off this morning. Alone in the elevator, she used the gleaming brass doors as a mirror, eyeing her impeccable hair, her perfect makeup, her chic, uncreased, black dress and black-and-white plaid jacket. Everything passed inspection. She felt sure she looked the part of Assistant to the President of Wentworth Enterprises, and took a deep breath just as the elevator glided to a stop. A quiet woman's voice announced, "Penthouse level, forty-fifth floor, Wentworth Enterprises."

How nice to have an elevator speak to you in the morning, Lindsey thought dazedly. What would they come up with next? Croissants and espresso served by a dumbwaiter on the trip up?

She stepped off the elevator and headed for the glass doors with the firm's name inscribed in gold. The same receptionist who had greeted her a month ago, on the hottest day of the year, sat behind the massive mahogany desk. When she looked up, she smiled and greeted Lindsey by name:

"Ms. Andrews, welcome aboard. How nice to see you this morning."

Lindsey smiled and nodded, quickly scanning the desk to find the receptionist's nameplate. "Thank you, Mrs. Danvers. It's nice to be here."

"You're to report to Personnel first. Miss Peach will fill you in on benefits and that sort of thing. Then she'll bring you along to Mr. Wentworth's office."

"Miss Peach." Vaguely, Lindsey recalled a cartoon character of the same name and suppressed a sudden desire to giggle madly. She was nervous and didn't give a damn about

Miss Peach, the Personnel Department, or her benefits. She wanted to get to her office and begin her new job.

Then too, there was also the small matter of seeing Jed Wentworth again. She wondered how she would react to him, then momentarily forgot her questions as she found herself in Personnel, signing forms and selecting insurance benefits and designating beneficiaries. Lindsey listened to explanations about company policy and nodded patiently, smiling until she thought her face would crack. She took the royal tour and was introduced to everyone on the staff and realized immediately that she wouldn't remember a place, face or title ten minutes later.

It was all a blur. The only thing that seemed real was the expectation of approaching Jed Wentworth's office, of seeing him and finding out at last what it would be like to work side by side with him. As the tour continued, her nervousness returned, blossoming with each step, casting a shadow on her first day. She wished suddenly that she was back at comfortable little Peabody and Company, where she was a small fish in a small but very well-known pond.

By the time she was walking down the corridor toward Margaret Oliver's office, she was filled with doubt and apprehension. She'd been a fool to take this job. It was all a huge mistake. She didn't belong here. Jed was right—she didn't have the experience to handle the job, not even as his assistant. She was out of her league, in over her head. She was small potatoes in a mammoth dinner menu.

Thanking Miss Peach for the tour, Lindsey stopped outside Margaret Oliver's officer. She felt as if she were Marie Antoinette riding on the tumbril toward her death. The guillotine, in the form of Jed Wentworth, waited.

Lindsey swallowed uncomfortably and grasped the doorknob. Immediately her sweaty hand slid off. She wiped it on her dress and tried again. This time she was successful. The door swung open and Margaret Oliver looked up from her work.

"So you're here at last," the older woman said curtly.

"Yes," Lindsey replied, sinking into a chair. She glanced nervously at the doors to Jed's office. "Is he expecting me?"

"Of course," Margaret snapped. "But he's on a conference call now. You'll have to wait till he's finished."

Lindsey forced a smile, then unobtrusively wiped her palms on her dress again. Somehow Margaret Oliver made everything that much harder. She'd never been Lindsey's favorite person on earth, but she was rapidly becoming her least favorite. Margaret was about as welcoming as a slammed door. Right when Lindsey needed encouragement, she was getting the coldest shoulder in town.

Margaret looked up again, glaring over the frames of her glasses at the telephone. "Ah, he's off at last." She gave Lindsey a severe look, then buzzed Jed's office. "Mr. Wentworth? She's here." She nodded. "Yes, sir, I'll send her right in."

Margaret hung up and held a hand out toward Jed's office doors. "Well? What are you waiting for? A twenty-piece marching band to escort you in?"

Lindsey suppressed the desire to snap back and decided she'd have to learn to live with Margaret's curmudgeonly demeanor. Jed obviously liked it, because he put up with her, though for the life of her, Lindsey couldn't understand why.

Taking a deep breath, Lindsey walked toward her doom. She tapped timidly on the door, only to have Jed's robust voice boom out, "Come on in!"

At the sound of his voice, Lindsey went limp. Jed was in there, just behind those doors. Excitement burgeoned within her, making her tremble with expectation. Her head whirled. Was it the new job or seeing Jed that excited her?

"What are you waiting for?" Margaret asked dryly. "Christmas?"

Lindsey turned a dazed face to Margaret. "Oh." She laughed nervously. "I guess I can go in, huh?"

Margaret rested her chin in her hand and nodded slowly, eyes narrowed. "I guess you can. He's been anxious to see you, excited as a new pup. Every other minute he's been buzzing me. 'Where's Lindsey? Where's Lindsey?' If I were you, I wouldn't keep him waiting any longer."

Stupefied by this news, Lindsey turned and put her hand on the door, only to have it pulled open at the same time from the inside. She was catapulted into Jed's office and, in a move that completely unnerved her, landed in his arms. He slammed the door and in the next second was kissing her, hard.

She clung to him, returning his kiss measure for measure, her eyes closed in rapture, her body pressed against his, drinking him in as if she'd been dying of thirst for the past three weeks.

Jed was the first to come to his senses. He lifted his head and stared at her. "Lord have mercy," he said, sounding dazed, "what the hell are we doing?"

Lindsey shook her head blankly, unable to speak. The only sense that worked was touch, and it was working overtime. She was suddenly in full possession of the memory of Jed's warm skin under her hands, of the way he had massaged her back and shoulders that night they had worked late together. And now here she was again, in his arms before she'd even started her new job. Could there be any worse way to start off her first day? she wondered bleakly.

"I'll tell you what we're doing," Jed said, putting his hands on her shoulders and gently moving her about ten feet away. "We're forgetting that this is a business and we have work to do."

Lindsey was mortified. Her face went crimson. She stepped back another three feet and nervously fidgeted with her pocketbook. "I knew it was a mistake," she said without thinking. "I just knew it. It won't work. We'll ruin everything. I quit." She turned to go, only to have Jed's strong hand pull her up short.

"Ms. Andrews." His voice was filled with quiet authority, backed by about a ton of steel.

She stopped and turned to face him. "Yes?"

"You're not quitting. You haven't even begun. You can't quit if you haven't begun. You follow that logic, don't you?"

She nodded, again at a loss for words.

"Can you speak, Ms. Andrews?"

"Argh—" She cleared her throat, then backed farther away. She felt safer when at least six feet separated her and Jed Wentworth. "Why of course I can speak, Mr. Wentworth," she said brightly.

He seemed to relax. He took a medium-deep breath and shoved his hands into his trouser pockets. "Your new office is through there," he said, gesturing at an open door. "It connects with mine, as you can see."

She nodded.

He sighed and raked a hand through his hair. "Ms. Andrews, please go into your office and compose yourself. Comb your hair. Repair your lipstick, and for heaven's sake, get a hold of yourself. This is a job you've just taken on, not an invitation to a prom."

Lindsey stared at him, then slowly began to relax. He could have taken advantage of her. She wouldn't have stopped him—couldn't have in her condition. But instead he was being just a little gruff and disapproving, goading her, forcing her to step into her new role and forget what had just happened between them. Okay, she thought, turning on her heel. She'd do just that.

"I must say, Mr. Wentworth," she said at the door to her office. "That greeting at the door was a *mite* overdone."

A flicker of a smile appeared on his face, then just as quickly disappeared. "Believe me, Ms. Andrews, it will never happen again."

"I should hope not," she said curtly, then disappeared into her office and slammed the door after her. It was a particularly effective exit. Suddenly, she felt right at home.

Eight

There's a meeting at 3:00 p.m. and I expect you to be there," Jed said, towering over her desk.

Lindsey stabbed the report she was writing with her pen. "And *I* am writing a report! I will *not* be bullied into going to some ridiculous committee meeting where no one does anything but shoot the proverbial breeze. Honestly, Jed, we've discussed this before. There's just not any point in both of us attending the same meetings. I can read the minutes later or you can fill me in."

"I want you there."

"And what Jed Wentworth wants, Jed Wentworth gets, is that it?"

"Something like that."

Their eyes locked. Lindsey looked away first. There was something steely about Jed's eyes today. For the past month, they had tiptoed around each other, being absurdly polite, extra careful not to let personal feelings interfere with work. But today Jed seemed to be pulling rank. Lindsey sighed and put down her pen.

"All right," she said wearily. "Where is it?"

"In my office. I expect you there. On time." With that, Jed turned and walked out, slamming the door after him.

It had gotten to be a habit between them. Either Lindsey slammed the door or he did. She didn't think the door had been closed quietly once in the entire month she'd worked there. It had become some kind of private signal between them, one she didn't want to examine too closely. Personally, she thought it symbolized the pent-up tension that simmered between them. Every time she or Jed slammed the door, it was a reminder that they really wanted to forget work and fall into each others' arms.

Lindsey wondered if a short, discreet affair mightn't be the answer. Maybe if they got it out of their systems they'd be able to put the silly attraction behind them and get on with work.

Sighing, Lindsey looked around the office. In the month she'd been here, she'd already grown to love it. Pale mauve carpeting covered the floor. White couches heaped with mauve and lavender pillows sat at right angles in a corner, with a huge glass-topped table scattered with business magazines in the middle. The white walls held a few cool abstract paintings done in mauve, pink, ivory and soft lavender. And behind her white desk, an entire wall of windows looked out over Hartford and its suburbs, spread before her like a vast visual feast.

But she had to admit that it wasn't the office that brought her bright-eyed to work every morning. While she loved the plush surroundings, she adored her work, and perhaps the most exciting part of that work was interacting with Jed Wentworth.

He was a dynamo. He worked ten-hour days regularly with no sign of strain. He alternately laughed, swore, threw things and cajoled, but he ultimately always got his way. Everyone loved him, and Lindsey was beginning to wonder if that didn't include her, too.

Rubbing her eyes, Lindsey swiveled her chair to take in the expansive view. It was early September. Soon the leaves would begin to change color and she would have a bird's-eye view from forty-five stories up. But the state of the landscape wasn't what really concerned her; the state of her heart was.

Little by little, inch by inch, she was falling for Jed. She knew it, couldn't deny it to herself any longer. The physical attraction she felt for him was overpowering, yet so far she had been able to stifle it, to pretend it didn't exist. But there was a far more potent attraction simmering inside her—an attraction to the man himself, to the energy and vision and determination he brought to every aspect of his work, to his enthusiasm, his sense of humor, his kindness, his concern for safety, for quality work, for the future of Hartford.

As she had worked by his side for the past month, she'd begun to realize that Jed Wentworth was a man of principle. He wasn't just in this for the buck; he was doing what he loved, and consequently money seemed to flow to him, as naturally as salmon swim upstream. He had found a slight design flaw in one of the buildings for the river-development project and had sent it back to be redesigned. The engineers had protested, telling him the flaw was minor, something that could be corrected on the job.

"Gentlemen," Jed had said, "no design flaw is minor. It goes back to the drawing board. We won't cut any corners with this project. When The Connecticut River Plaza is finished, it'll be the safest complex known to man. We're not going to have another Civic Center here," he added, referring to Hartford's first Civic Center roof, which had collapsed early one morning in 1978 under a two-foot covering of hard-packed ice and snow.

"Come on, Jed," Ron Dempsey, the senior engineer, had said, "this isn't anywhere near that bad a flaw. It's so minor it's almost undetectable."

Jed merely rolled up the engineering drawings and handed them to Ron. "Do them over," he said tersely.

Ron had sighed, then nodded. "You're the boss."

"That's right. I am."

Watching from the sidelines, Lindsey had felt her admiration for Jed take a quantum leap. Jed's principles would not be compromised, nor would the safety of the citizens of Hartford. Suddenly, just working for him, she felt safer. Instinctively, she knew she could trust him. And along with those feelings of safety and trust, came something else, something warmer, deeper, a feeling filled with fire and fierceness. She hadn't wanted to name it then, because it scared her too much, but now, sitting at her desk, looking out over the Connecticut River as it wended its way down from Springfield, Massachusetts, she knew what it was: the first stirring of love.

Shaken by this insight, Lindsey groaned and swiveled back to her desk. She didn't want things to get even more complicated. Just the physical attraction was difficult enough to deal with. How could she handle falling in love with her boss?

She slapped her hands on her desk and stood up. She couldn't. Thus, she wouldn't. It was as simple as that. Mind over matter. Willpower. Self-control. Call it what she would, she was determined to nip this feeling in the bud. She'd continue to respect Jed, continue to like him, but she was damned if she'd fall in love with him.

After all, Jed Wentworth wasn't the kind of man a sane woman fell in love with. He was a known philanderer, a heartbreaker, a wooer of beautiful women, and most important, a confirmed bachelor. If a man hadn't married by thirty-eight, he wasn't going to, or at least that was Lindsey's philosophy. It had certainly been borne out by her old boyfriend Ken Lawson. He was past forty now and still hadn't settled down. The last she heard, he was dating three women at the same time and sleeping with all of them. So much for the need for Safe Sex. With Ken Lawson, sex was as necessary as air and water. She suspected Jed Wentworth was cut from the same cloth.

Ever practical, Lindsey gathered her notebook and shooed away the pang in her heart. She'd get over Jed in a few more weeks. This attraction was a momentary aberration, one she would handle with a dash of humor and a hands-off approach.

She slipped into Jed's office a minute after three, only to have him give her a dark look, "You're late, Ms. Andrews."

"Only a minute, Mr. Wentworth."

"A minute too much," he said, then continued with the meeting agenda.

Lindsey sat and simmered. A few of the committee members had tittered at the exchange, and she didn't like that. Jed always came out on top. Just once, she'd like to best him at his own game.

"Ms. Andrews..." Jed's voice cut into her musings. "Are you taking notes?"

"Oh..." She felt her face grow pink and opened her steno pad. "Yes, sir."

She began to write down what was happening. Soon she was lost in a labyrinth of politicking and internal maneuverings. Peter Gibson, new Director for Publicity and Advertising, was calling for a consolidated public relations campaign. He presented some mock-ups of the suggested brochures. Jed glanced through them, then pushed them toward Lindsey. "I'd like a complete report on these brochures on my desk in the morning, Ms. Andrews."

"Yes, sir."

"Why do you need a report from Lindsey?" Peter Gibson asked. "You can see for yourself what I'm getting at here."

"I don't have the time to study them in depth, Pete," Jed explained. "That's Lindsey's job."

Peter Gibson looked over at Lindsey speculatively. She kept her eyes down, scribbling nonsense on her notepad, but at the end of the meeting, Peter Gibson was beside her in ten seconds. "Lindsey, we haven't really talked much," he said, extending his hand. "Why don't we have a drink sometime?"

Slightly surprised, Lindsey smiled and nodded. "That would be great, Peter. It would give us a chance to talk about your plans for the project."

"Exactly. How about tonight?"

Lindsey laughed musically. "Now come on. You expect me to be Superwoman? Jed just asked for a complete report on your brochures by tomorrow morning. Uh-uh. Afraid tonight's out. Some other time, though."

"Tomorrow night, then."

Feeling slightly pushed, Lindsey begged off. "Sorry, Pete. I've got other plans." She softened her rejection with a warm smile. "Call me sometime next week and we'll get together."

"It's a date," said Peter Gibson, smiling.

"Lindsey, I'd like to see you before you leave," Jed called out.

Turning, she looked at Jed. "Yes?"

"I like the way you shook off Gibson," Jed said when the doors had closed on the last of the committee members.

"Shook him off? What do you mean?"

"He's obviously making a play for you. As soon as he found out how important your input is to me, he decided to move in and get up close and personal. Watch yourself,

Lindsey. You just might find yourself fending off more men than you bargained on."

She didn't know why she did it, but some devil made her say, "Peter Gibson is quite nice looking. Who says I'll want to fend him off?"

The smile on Jed's face gradually faded. "Are you purposely goading me, Lindsey?" he asked softly.

"Goading you?" she asked innocently. "Why, not at all."

He nodded slowly. "I'd like that report extra early tomorrow morning," he said, going back to his work.

"How early?"

"Six a.m."

"Six a.m.!" she echoed. "Are you *crazy*?"

He didn't even bother to look up. "Six a.m.," he said, patting the surface of his desk. "Right here. Typed, double-spaced, no errors."

"You—"

He looked up. "Yes? What were you going to call me?"

She boiled. "Simon Legree," she said, then stomped into her office and *really* slammed the door.

Lindsey sat on her couch sipping a cup of soup, her feet snuggled under her. She'd had a quick shower when she'd gotten home, slipped into a comfortable robe, and then sat down with the material from the office. She was so immersed in reading the mock-ups of the brochures Peter Gibson had designed, her forehead was creased with concentration and she'd forgotten what time it was.

Finally she put the last one down and stared at the crackling fire in her fireplace. They weren't right. It was a subtle thing, but they seemed to miss the point that Jed was striving so hard for. Yet she couldn't put her finger on what was wrong. The artwork was certainly first-rate, the writing was professional and competent, but something vital was missing, something indefinable. She didn't know what it was, but she'd know it if she saw it. Unfortunately, in all the brochures she'd looked over tonight, she hadn't seen it.

Yet how could she communicate that in her report to Jed? She glanced at the clock and saw that it was after 9:00 p.m. He wanted a complete report by 6:00 a.m., which left her less than nine hours, yet she hadn't a clue what to say—that they were good, but not right? Professional, but not quite good enough?

Groaning, she began doodling on her notepad, trying to come up with the elusive extra that was missing from the brochures. When the doorbell rang, at first it didn't register. She continued staring at her notepad, vaguely wondering what that bell was.

Then it hit her and she stared at the entry hall, puzzled. It was after 9:00 p.m. Who would be calling now? She went to the door and peered through the peephole. Astounded, she saw Peter Gibson staring back at her.

"Now, why is *he* here?" she whispered out loud, then remembered Jed's warning.

Immediately she rejected the idea that Peter Gibson would start wooing her. He probably just wanted to talk about the brochures. She opened the front door and smiled pleasantly.

"Hello, Peter, what brings you to this neighborhood?"

His brown eyes skimmed over her appreciatively. "You," he said, smiling and holding up a bottle of champagne. "I thought you might need a break from that report you're working on."

A warning bell went off in her mind, but she decided she'd give him the benefit of the doubt. "I sure don't need any champagne, but you're welcome to come in since you're here. I have a couple questions about the brochure, as a matter of fact. Maybe we can talk about them."

"Great!"

Peter was tall and blond, with brown eyes, a straight nose and a square chin. He was a very attractive man. She knew he was divorced and had left two kids in Chicago with his ex-wife.

She picked up one of the brochures and hesitated, trying to come up with the right words to explain her feelings.

"How do you like them?" Peter asked exuberantly. "They're great, huh?"

"Well..." she said slowly, "I think they're on the right track but may need to be refined a little. Something's not quite right. Maybe we can figure it out together."

"Not quite right?" Peter chuckled and popped the cork on the bottle. Making himself at home, he went to a wall cabinet, took out two glasses and poured some champagne. "Lindsey, I know you've done a little public relations and advertising work, but you haven't had anywhere near the experience I have. Trust me, these are good. They're top-notch stuff. Perhaps you need a little instruction in how a real professional works."

Lindsey stared at him. His arrogance astounded her. The man hadn't even let her express her opinion before telling her she didn't know what she was talking about! And to make matters worse, he was making himself entirely too much at home. He held out a glass of champagne to her as if he lived there, not she!

He sipped the champagne and smiled at her. "Come on, Lindsey, have a little champagne. Loosen up. Let old Pete give you a few lessons in publicity campaigns."

"Old Pete?" she asked dryly, taking the champagne and sipping it. "What are you—thirty-five? Does seven years give you that much of an edge on me, Peter?"

"Oh, come on, honey," Peter said. "Don't get riled now. That's a typical women's libber's reaction. Let a man with a little more experience come along and she gets all bent out of shape."

"I'm not bent out of shape."

Peter smiled easily. "Then let's have a friendlier meeting, shall we?" His eyes again skimmed her figure. "I think I'd like to be a lot friendlier with you."

"Would you?" she asked, anger slowly beginning to pump through her veins.

Peter smiled and took her arm. "Come on, let's stop talking business for a few minutes, okay? Let's get to know each other on a more personal level."

Lindsey eased her arm from his grip and smiled dryly. "I really don't think that's necessary, Peter. We can work together without having to get personal, don't you think?"

Peter stared at her thoughtfully and seemed to realize he was taking the wrong tack. He started over. "Lindsey, I've been admiring you from afar this past month. I think you've got spunk and a good brain."

"Thank you," she said quietly, beginning to dislike Peter Gibson more and more. When seducing her didn't work, he resorted to flattery.

Peter stared at her, then nodded, his smile suddenly gone. He looked tough and ready to fight. "Okay. Let's get down to business. Those brochures are my babies, Lindsey. I want to know what you're going to say about them in that report to Jed."

"Then you'll have to wait and find out from him."

"Lindsey, if you cross me on this thing, you'll regret it."

"I have no intention of 'crossing' you, as you put it," she said, setting down the champagne and picking up the array of brochures. "I want to work with you, Peter, not against you, but something's just not right here."

"Great!" Peter said, clearly exasperated. "What the hell is wrong with Jed, putting someone in charge of reporting on something she doesn't know anything about?"

"But I do know what I'm talking about, Peter," Lindsey said quietly. "I know quite a bit about publicity campaigns and advertising brochures. These are top-notch professional brochures, beautifully done, but the flavor's wrong. It's vanilla, when we need something more along the line of New England Dutch Chocolate. These brochures could be advertising any new development project in any city in the country. We need a brochure that captures the spirit of Jed's project, the individuality of it, the flavor of Connecticut and New England. Yes, it's cosmopolitan and sophisticated, but it's also in Hartford, not in San Francisco or Seattle or Detroit. Do you see what I'm getting at?"

"What do you want me to do, Lindsey?" Peter asked sarcastically. "Paint little red lobsters and bean pots along the edges to give it the 'flavor' of New England?"

His question hung in the air between them. Lindsey stared at him, then flipped the brochures on the coffee table. "Maybe you need to take a drive some weekend, Peter, and get to know Connecticut a little better. Maybe that would help you see what I'm talking about."

"I *know* what you're talking about, Lindsey. You're talking about cutesy little homespun slogans and colonial lettering." He visibly shuddered. "It won't work, Lindsey. This project is *not* cute, it's sophisticated. Take it from me, honey, those brochures are the best you're going to see."

"Then we're in trouble."

Again they glared at each other, friction vibrating in the air between them. They both jumped when the doorbell rang, shattering the tension with its sudden clamor.

"Lord!" Lindsey said, heading for the door. "*Now* who's here?" She didn't bother to look through the peephole, but flung the door open, then simply stared.

Jed Wentworth stared back at her, then looked past her at Peter Gibson. Jed seemed to take in everything in an instant—Lindsey's casual attire, the fire crackling romantically in the fireplace, the bottle of champagne, the half-empty glasses, and the suspicious presence of Peter Gibson.

Jed looked back at Lindsey, his eyes shimmering with unspoken questions. Lindsey felt her heart stop for a frightening moment, then heard it thundering in her breast. All kinds of disastrous scenarios played themselves out in her fertile imagination. Jed would fire her. He'd fire Peter. He'd fire both of them. From where he stood, things must look awfully incriminating.

She muttered under her breath, "Jed, believe me, it's not what you think...."

Nine

Then what, pray tell, is it?'' Jed asked quietly, closing the door.

''Not what it looks like,'' Lindsey whispered, then turned and smiled at Peter. ''Look who's here,'' she said brightly. ''A referee.''

Jed looked at her with narrowed eyes. ''Have I happened on a lover's quarrel, then?'' he suggested mildly.

''Peter stopped by very unexpectedly,'' Lindsey said, eyeing Jed coolly. ''I'm afraid we got into a bit of a heated discussion concerning his brochures.''

''I wouldn't really call it heated, Lindsey,'' Peter Gibson said, looking carefully from Lindsey to Jed. He smiled charmingly. ''It's just that Lindsey is having trouble understanding the concept I'm going after. It's rather sophisticated stuff for someone with Lindsey's limited experience.'' He looked from Jed to Lindsey, a twinkle in his eyes. ''But then maybe Lindsey's experience isn't as limited as I'd first thought."

The implication that Jed was here for personal reasons wasn't lost on Lindsey. She shot a quick look at Jed, who merely looked amused. Lifting her chin, she faced Peter Gibson squarely. "If it's my *business* experience in question here, you're correct," she said sharply. "It's not all that limited."

"Look," Peter said, holding up his hands, "it's getting late. Perhaps I should be going and let you two get down to whatever business it is you need to discuss." He smiled smoothly and shook Jed's hand, then nodded at Lindsey. "I hope we can discuss the brochures more fully tomorrow," he said, then looked at Jed. "I'll want to discuss Lindsey's report with you. I think she's very competent, but perhaps she needs to work a little more closely with me to get the hang of how things are done on high-level stuff."

"I'm sure Lindsey will be amenable to that," Jed said, eyeing her sardonically.

She glared at him, then showed Peter to the door and turned back to Jed. "Well?" she said sharply. "What are you here for?"

"Strange," Jed said, picking up the bottle of champagne and sniffing it. "That was my exact question regarding Pete Gibson."

"I *told* you," Lindsey said, exasperated, "it's not what it looked like. He stopped by and surprised the living daylights out of me. You were right, though—he did try to make a pass at me." She gestured to the champagne. "It didn't work, I'm afraid."

"Wrong brand?" asked Jed, wryly arching a brow as he examined the champagne label.

She gave him a seething look. "No, wrong man."

"Well, that gives me hope, at least."

"Don't let it," she retorted. "As far as you're concerned, there isn't any."

Jed sighed and sat down on the couch. He picked up a brochure and idly flipped through it. "You look very fetching in that fuzzy thing. Are you sure I didn't happen on, er—" Jed coughed delicately "—after-dinner drinks?"

Lindsey's green eyes burned with suppressed anger, but she refused to rise to the bait. "I came home, ate supper, and then started working on that damn report you ordered me to do. The doorbell rang a little after nine. It was Peter. He had the champagne and suggested we discuss the brochures. What was I supposed to do? Go out on the front porch to have our little talk?"

"I might have found that a bit more reassuring."

"You don't need to be reassured about anything," Lindsey said. "What I do in my personal life is my own business and no one else's."

"If what you do in your personal life involves another employee of mine," Jed countered acidly, "then it sure as hell *is* my business. If you're not fooling around with me, Lindsey, then you're not going to fool around with anyone who works for me."

"Of all the colossal gall," she breathed. "This takes the cake. What I do with my own life is none of your damn business, Jed Wentworth. Remember that."

Jed rose slowly from the couch. "I only remember one thing, Lindsey, something you seem to have forgotten—what happened between us when we worked late together one night. If it happened with me, it could happen with Peter."

"Nothing happened with Peter," she snapped. "And whatever happened between us that night no longer matters. That was before I even worked for you. It was late and we were tired. We both agreed it would never happen again."

"The trouble is, it *did* happen, and we both liked it, too. A lot. But I promised you I wouldn't persist in going after a personal involvement if that's not what you wanted. But after tonight's little debacle—"

"I *told* you," Lindsey cried, "nothing happened!"

"Then this is to make sure nothing does." Jed drew her into his arms. Before she could stop him, he was kissing her, his lips almost savage, his body bending over hers, imprinting it with the lean, hard contours of his.

Lindsey fought the kiss at first, but that seemed to fuel Jed's passion. "Stop it, Lindsey," he murmured, looking deeply into her eyes. "Stop fighting it and just once give in to it. Kiss me. Kiss me the way you kissed me that night in the office, the way you kissed me the first day on the job."

She stared into his eyes, frightened by the bald words he spoke. It had been safe before, when everything was unsaid. Now she felt as if the scenery had been pulled down and the play was over. Suddenly they were no longer acting. This was real.

"Don't talk that way," she insisted. "I don't want to kiss you!"

"I think you do," Jed said softly. "Shall I prove it to you?"

She moaned weakly, turning her head away, but he pressed his face against the side of her neck, brushing against the soft skin, breathing heatedly into her ear, his nose nudging her, urging her to respond. "Kiss me, Lindsey," he murmured. "Kiss me."

She trembled, and found her arms slowly going around him, clinging to him, found her head nuzzling into his chest, found herself lifting her neck so that his lips could caress the soft skin under her ear. She gasped softly and melted into his embrace. "What are you doing to me?" she whispered, her eyes closed in ecstacy as his lips captured the lobe of her ear.

"Showing you what it could be like," he murmured, letting his lips travel over her neck. His hands moved up and down her back, pressing her into his hardness. "Feel it, Lindsey," he whispered, his tongue flicking fire into her ear. "Feel every bit of it."

She ran her hands up his back and around his neck, clinging to him, going up on tiptoe to seek out his lips. "Kiss me," she whispered shakily. "Hurry. Kiss me."

His lips took warm possession of hers, sucking the strength from her body until she had melted against him, all willingness now, no longer fighting but begging for his embrace.

"Yes," she whispered between kisses. "Oh, yes!" She returned kiss for kiss. His hands held her head, tipped it back and he kissed her softly, gently, nibbled at her lips, probed and questioned and made her melt with longing.

"You see?" he murmured when at last they broke apart. "Do you see how it could be with us?"

She saw. Having experienced Jed's kisses, having savored the warmth of his embrace, she now knew what she was denying herself. Yet she had to. Because for Jed, this was just another fling with an attractive woman, someone new to conquer before he moved on to new game. This was the hunt to Jed; it was the game he played and won. But for Lindsey, it would mean ruin.

Her gaze fell on the brochures for the riverfront-development project. She saw the architects' sketches, saw the soaring buildings and the proposed conference center, and knew she had to continue her dream. It was her father's dream, too, had been his from the very beginning, even before there was a Jed Wentworth.

And all of it would die if she gave in to a few hours of bliss with Jed. She folded her arms and smiled cynically. "You almost got me, Jed," she said ironically. "The fatal

Wentworth charm almost worked. But the sincere approach ruined things."

Jed tilted his head and studied her. "The sincere approach?"

"You know, the sincere questions: 'Do you see how it could be with us, Lindsey?'" She snorted. "What bothers me is that I almost fell for it! You really did sound sincere! For a minute there, I was a sitting duck. Thank God I came to my senses and realized who I was with."

"You really think I'm some kind of Don Juan, don't you?" he asked, shaking his head as if trying to comprehend where she was coming from.

"Yes, I do!" she shot back. "Honestly, Jed, you'd try to lure the clothes off a photograph if the woman was pretty enough."

"What if I told you I really cared about you?"

"I'd consider it a new line from a master seducer."

He shoved a hand back through his hair and shook his head again, then began pacing back and forth, his hands on his hips. "I can't win with you, can I, Andrews? You've got it into your head I'm a skirt-chaser and that's the end, isn't it? No more evidence needed. Judge and jury have decided: Jed Wentworth is guilty and the trial is over."

"Look, let's leave personalities out of it. Let's just look at this thing practically. For you, it's no big deal. A new woman, a new challenge. But for *me*..."

"Yes, what about you, Lindsey?" Jed challenged. "After the way you kissed me just now, you can't expect me to believe you're made out of bolts and baling wire. I just held a warm, responsive woman. What are you running from?"

"I'm running, as you call it, from certain disaster!" she cried, beginning to tremble from anger. "I can't risk getting involved with you. This job means too much to me."

"And I'm telling you that the job isn't at risk, Lindsey," Jed said. "You can have both. The job *and* me."

She stared at him, stymied. "Jed," she said quietly, "I want to do it on my own. I thought you'd understand that. I don't know much about you, but I do know you came out of nowhere and made it big. No one helped you. No one gave you a leg up the corporate ladder. You built it yourself, rung by rung. Can't you understand that I might feel that way, too? That I've also got to prove myself to myself?"

He stared at the rug, his face in shadows, then he shrugged. "Okay, if that's how you want it, that's how it'll be." He picked up the bottle of champagne. "You gonna finish this?"

She shook her head. Champagne was the last thing she wanted now. Champagne was for celebrating, and she had nothing to celebrate, even though she'd won what she wanted.

"Then I'll just take it along," Jed said, taking a healthy swig from the bottle. His eyes sparkled as he looked down at her. "And you, my dear, have a report due on my desk at six tomorrow morning." Grinning at the look on her face, he turned and walked toward the front door. "See you in the morning," he said. "Six a.m., sharp."

He closed the door and she was suddenly alone. She slumped back on the couch and stared at the champagne that had gone flat in the two glasses. For the first time in her life, she wondered if her principles were just a little bit *too* pure....

Lindsey dashed into the high-speed elevator that whisked her to the top floor, then headed straight for Jed's office. It was five minutes of six, and the report she'd prepared was steaming in her briefcase.

She pushed open the door to his office and came to a complete stop. Jed was seated at his desk, immersed in paperwork. She hadn't expected to see him here. His presence so early in the day startled her. She wondered if he was here this early every morning.

Then he looked up and she knew the answer. He wasn't always here this early. Today was unique. His face was lined with fatigue and she realized he was wearing the same suit and shirt he'd worn last night at her town house.

Her heart was wrenched with anguish at the sight of him. She felt an overpowering desire to go to him and smooth back his rumpled hair, to stroke his temples, to massage his tense neck and shoulders. Everything in her cried out to him, but he stopped her cold when he spoke to her. His voice was as impersonal as a computer.

"Well, I see you made the deadline, Ms. Andrews. Good work." He indicated a clear spot on his desk. "Put the report there, please, and I'll get to it when I can."

She faltered for just a moment, then mustered the same impersonal tone he'd used. "Yes, sir," she said, dropping the report on his desk and trying to suppress nervous butterflies of apprehension as she did so. What would he think of it? It was, to put it mildly, short, succinct, and to the point.

She turned on her heel and headed to her office. "Did you work all night, Mr. Wentworth?"

"Mmmm," he said, obviously already reimmersed in his work.

She looked back at him and noted the tired slump of his strong shoulders and again felt the urge to go to him. But he had erected a wall that seemed insurmountable. Standing only fifteen feet away from him, she felt as if she were on the edge of the Pacific Ocean and he on the edge of the Atlantic. A continent separated them.

Staring at him, Lindsey felt an intense sense of loss. Would it be this way between them from now on? Cold, impersonal, businesslike and efficient? Her heart sank, and then she realized the irony of the situation. This was what she had wanted, had actually demanded of Jed. But now that he was complying with her wishes, she didn't like it. She wanted to go back to the bickering and sparring. Fighting verbally had been their safety valve. Angry outbursts at each other had allowed the sexual tension between them to dissipate without doing any harm. She realized now, too late, it had been exciting to work with Jed not just because the *work* was exciting but also because of the undercurrents that threatened to flare between them.

Feeling dazed by the rush of sudden insights, Lindsey turned and went into her office. For the first time, she didn't slam the door. She felt too sick, too filled with regret and longing. What had she thrown away last night? What precious chemistry had she destroyed with her rigidity and high principles?

Blindly, she went to the wide expanse of windows behind her desk. Dawn was just breaking. There was a narrow band of brilliant light on the eastern horizon, yet stars still lingered in the sky above. She sank into her chair and watched the slow but inexorable spread of light. Then the top rim of the sun itself appeared, rising like a giant beast from its sleep, creeping up and peeking over the edge of the world.

She wondered if it liked what it saw. Was it ever tempted, upon first viewing the prodigious folly of mankind, to climb back down and head eastward again, to bury itself behind the horizon and seek shelter from the foolishness of human beings?

Groaning, she swiveled and rested her elbows on her desk, putting her head in her hands. What was she doing with her life? What meaning would it have ten years from now, or twenty? If she threw herself headlong into her work, when would she have time for a relationship with a man, for marriage and children?

Until now, she hadn't given them a thought. They were peripheral to her existence, to her compulsive need to prove her mother wrong and show her up, while carrying on in her dead father's name. When the White Knight had fallen, she had picked up his lance, but now she wondered if his fight was really hers. What good would come of carrying a grudge? Twenty years from now, when she was alone at the top of some corporation, would she be comforted by the memories of her father? Would she regret having shut her mother out of her life? Would she miss the warmth of a family around the hearth? Would holidays like Thanksgiving and Christmas become empty hours, spent with only remorse as company?

Lindsey clenched her hands and squeezed her eyes shut. She needed answers and all she had was questions. Instinctively, she knew she was meant to work. As a career woman, all her intelligence and energy had gone into her job. But she was also a woman. What had she done for that womanly part of herself lately?

Then her door banged open and Jed appeared, miraculously rejuvenated. "What the hell is this?" he demanded, waving a piece of paper at her.

"It looks as if it's my report," she said dryly, but, inside, her heart was pumping with excitement and renewed hope. Jed was alive again! They were fighting!

He gave her a bleak stare, then began reading out loud: "Artwork: first-class. Writing: professional, competent, lucid. Overall impression: Something's missing. Recommendation: Back to the drawing board."

She winced at the hard tone of voice he used, but managed a bright smile when he looked up at her. His pale eyes were filled with lively sparks. "This isn't a report," he said wryly. "It's a damn *outline*!"

She shrugged. "It's all I thought was necessary. It conveys my message. If you don't trust my judgment, maybe you'd better find a new assistant."

He stared at her, then sat down in a chair facing her desk. Slowly, he put his feet up on her desk top, establishing immediate control over her space. He laced his fingers together and placed them behind his head. To her amazement, he smiled.

"I like it," he said. "It's the first time in fifteen years anyone's had the nerve to write a concise memo that's not filled with pages of padded garbage. And—" he tilted his head and surveyed her speculatively "—I just happen to agree with you. Something *isn't* right in those brochures. I'm damned if I can put my finger on it, but I know what you're talking about. I feel it, too."

"Oh, Jed!" she said, elation flooding her. "I'm so happy I could kiss you!"

One corner of his mouth twitched in lazy amusement. "I think that might not be in the best interests of either of our sanities, Ms. Andrews." He rose and strolled toward his door, then looked back at her, eyes sparkling with humor. "Still, if you ever get the urge to go a little crazy, I'm right next door."

She broke into a radiant smile. "I'll remember that, Mr. Wentworth."

"I sincerely hope you do," he said, then carefully closed the door.

Ten

Peter Gibson leaned over Lindsey's desk, his nose thrust aggressively toward hers, his knuckles white from the pressure he exerted on the desk top.

"And I tell you there's not a damn thing wrong with those brochures!" he shouted, his face mottled with color. "They're dynamite. They're sophisticated and metropolitan and classy. Dammit, Lindsey, they're first-rate professional stuff, but that ridiculous three-line report you gave to Jed ruined everything." He raked his hand back through his immaculately combed hair and sighed heavily. "What the hell am I supposed to make of this?" he asked, reading from Lindsey's report, "'Something's missing?'"

Lindsey shrugged. "Jed agrees with me. Something's missing. Neither of us can put our finger on it, but whatever it is, it's not there."

"Can you give me a clue?" Peter asked acidly. "Is it bigger than a bread box, for instance? Is there a word missing, a sentence, an entire paragraph? Are we talking pictures or words here? Would you like pretty little stars around the title line?''

''Peter, I tried to tell you last night—it's the *tone* that's wrong, the flavor of the entire concept. It's metropolitan, yes, and it's sophisticated and classy, and we want all that, but we want something else, too, something that's entirely different, that spells Connecticut, that makes these brochures stand out as much as the Riverfront Plaza will. It's image we're talking here, Peter. You haven't captured it yet.''

''Image?'' he snorted. ''Connecticut hasn't *got* an image! Fairfield County's got an image—money, and lots of it. Litchfield County's got an image—scenic beauty, rustic trees—you know, the beautiful New England, covered-bridge scene, but Connecticut itself doesn't stand for anything. Particularly Hartford.'' He snorted again. ''The insurance capital of the world! My God, how utterly boring!''

''That's what we're asking you to do, Peter,'' Lindsey said quietly: ''Come up with an image for Connecticut. No one else has been able to do it so far. We're counting on your expertise to do the trick.''

Lindsey watched as Peter's face began to change slowly from contempt to interest. He stroked his chin thoughtfully, then began to pace. ''Yes,'' he said slowly, ''I see. An image for Connecticut...''

Lindsey hid her smile. She'd done it—she'd managed to engage Peter Gibson's considerable ego. Instead of turning him off and offending him, she'd presented him with a challenge.

Peter went to stand at the windows overlooking Hartford and its surroundings. The trees were beginning to change color, heralding the coming of autumn. ''What's Connecticut got that other states don't?'' he asked as if to himself, staring at the river that wound peacefully through the Connecticut River Valley, bisecting the state. He turned to Lindsey. "What *does* Connecticut have that other states don't?" he asked, this time truly interested.

"History," Lindsey answered promptly, "and beauty and scenery like you've never seen. I meant it when I said take a drive sometime, Peter. Head east from Hartford. When I was growing up, it was all tobacco land, part of the incredibly fertile Connecticut River Valley, which produced the best broad-leaf tobacco in the world. You can still see some of those wonderful old tobacco barns, with the weathered wood and the sides that opened for ventilation. They dot the landscape all over South and East Windsor and Windsor Locks and Suffield and Granby. Every summer, all the teenagers in central Connecticut worked tobacco. It was a way of life that's vanishing. Now they bring in workers from Puerto Rico every summer for the few tobacco farms still producing."

Lindsey warmed to her subject, her eyes glowing. "Take a drive out to South Windsor and look at the Congregational Church at Five Corners. You sit there at the traffic light and suddenly, as if by magic, the twentieth century falls away and you're back in the 1800s, looking at one of the best examples of Colonial architecture in the country. That church dominates the landscape. Its steeple soars to the sky. Huge trees dot the front lawn. It's got everything that Connecticut and New England stand for—simplicity and beauty and a kind of spirituality that just isn't found in today's architecture."

She took a breath and went on, afraid Peter would interrupt. "And then, when you're finished looking at the church, drive down Route 194 and cross over Route 5 and go down Old Main Street in South Windsor. Peter, it's the most beautiful old street you'll ever want to see. Litchfield's more famous for its main street, but I swear the houses you'll see here are just as impressive. There are lots of old, weathered, redbrick houses, built back in the early 1800s. The trees climb halfway to the sky. There's a serenity and peacefulness you just can't find anywhere else on earth. And behind it all lies the Connecticut River—muddy-looking, yes, and not as huge and impressive as the Mississippi, but majestic in its own way. Slow-moving, steady, calm, like the people who settled Connecticut. A wise old river, still here after all these years."

Peter stared at her. "You love it, don't you?"

Lindsey turned to look out the window at the sweeping vista. "Yes," she mused, "I guess I do. Maybe I didn't realize just how much until now."

"History," Peter said slowly. "I think that's what's coming through. A sense of time, of steady, uninterrupted progress while not turning one's back on the past."

Lindsey began to smile. Foolish tears misted her sentimental eyes. "That's it," she said softly. "You're getting it, Peter. Your brochures showed soaring new skyscrapers that could be part of any modern, cosmopolitan city, but we're not just any city, Peter, we're Hartford. We're different here. We're old *and* new, we've got history and scenic beauty and a past that shines in history books. We can't forget that, Peter. We can't lose track of the past. It made us what we are. We go on, we change, we continue to grow, yes, but we never forget to honor our history."

Peter pursed his lips and folded his arms and rocked back on his heels as he stared at the carpet. "I think I'm beginning to see. It wasn't hokey little red lobsters or colonial lettering you wanted on the brochures, was it?"

She shook her head, smiling at Peter as if at an old friend who'd come back after a long quarrel. "Nope."

"I'm sorry, Lindsey," he said quietly. "I guess the old professional needed to learn something from the young kid on the block."

"You've got everything you need to do the job, Peter," she said. "Except you didn't grow up in Hartford. You don't love it the way I do. You were lacking the heart, and I have that."

"Heart," he said, looking at her quizzically. "They don't teach that in business school, Lindsey. They teach advertising concepts and marketing techniques, but they leave out the heart."

"That's what's wrong with the world, Peter," Lindsey said. "The heart's being forgotten. In our desperate race to get more and build bigger, we've forgotten the only thing that really matters."

She swiveled away from him and pretended to look out the windows, her eyes misted again with ridiculous tears. Why couldn't she control them? Her silly little speech about heart had suddenly shown her what she'd done with her own life, and the knowledge hurt. She'd been finding out a lot about herself and her priorities lately, and everything she learned was vastly painful. Businesses weren't the only ones who'd shut the heart out of their existences; so had she. She'd become a driven woman, an automaton, bent on achieving her father's ambitions while punishing her mother.

Her personal life was a shambles. She didn't have one, as a matter of fact. She lived alone, without even the comfort of an animal's company. She had no lovers and few friends, but her closet was full of expensive clothes and she drove a shiny, new car. What had been *wrong* with her? When had she bought into the conventional wisdom that success and material possessions were all that mattered? She'd scorned her mother for those values, but realized now they were also her own.

"Peter?"

Turning she found that he had gone. She was alone in her spacious office. Alone yet again. She picked up a pencil and began to doodle. Later, coming to, she realized she'd filled the pad of paper with hearts, and in the middle of each were Jed Wentworth's initials.

Staring at them, she felt her world begin to crack apart. All the need and love and warmth she'd locked away at her father's death came pouring out in a rushing river of tears. They seemed a veritable flood, pouring from her very soul, leaving her shaken and weak and filled with desperation. She thought of going to Jed for comfort, but knew she couldn't. Lindsey needed to see her mother, needed to talk with her, needed to find out where she'd gone wrong these past ten years. How had she been so misguided? How had she let herself believe that any job on earth mattered more than human beings?

She picked up the phone and punched out her mother's number. Odd. In all these years, she'd never forgotten it. That alone was a clue to how much she'd needed her. She'd just never admitted it before.

Her mother answered, her voice firm and filled with good humor. "Hello?"

"Mother?"

There was a hesitation, then Eliza spoke with a mixture of fear and expectation. "Lindsey?"

"Yes. Um, I..."

"Are you all right, Lindsey?" Concern echoed in Eliza Cartwright's voice.

"Yes!" said Lindsey brightly. "It's just that I...I was wondering if I could come see you."

"Well, of course you can come see me!" Eliza said joyfully. "Come now! Come for supper!"

"Oh, no, I wouldn't stay for supper, it's just that I'd like to talk with you. I thought I'd stop by after work."

"Of course," Eliza said, "then come right along. I'll be here, waiting for you." She hesitated, then asked, "Do you still like tea with honey?"

The tears started again, but Lindsey managed to hold them in check. "Mmm-hmm," she murmured, her throat closing up so she couldn't speak.

"Well, it's a little nippy out, so I'll make a nice hot pot of tea and we'll have honey in it and, let's see, I have molasses cookies and hermits. You still like them, don't you? Or are you watching your figure?"

"I love molasses cookies and hermits," Lindsey said fervently, twisting the phone cord around her finger and holding back the tears that still threatened.

"Then come along," her mother said gently. "I'll be waiting for you."

Lindsey couldn't hang up. Her mother didn't, either. They both seemed to wait, suspended in time, then Lindsey said, "Thank you, Mother."

"Thank *you*, Lindsey."

Lindsey hung up quickly and gave way to the blasted onslaught of tears. Damn the things anyway—they seemed as unstoppable as a river....

The Cartwright house was a two-story brick building with shiny black shutters at the windows, just up from Prospect Street near Elizabeth Park. There was a circular driveway, carefully tended shrubs and a garden plot filled with colorful mums.

Lindsey pulled her car to a stop and got out, staring at the impressive facade of the house. She'd hated it from the moment she'd first seen it. To her, it represented everything wrong with her mother—ambition, going after material possessions, the desire to be rich and most damning of all, lack of loyalty.

Now she saw it was just a house, and she had probably resented it because her mother had it and she didn't. After her mother left, Lindsey had stayed with her father in the horrible old triple-decker filled with dark woodwork and

Victorian furniture. No light had ever penetrated that place. Here, sunshine seemed to surround the house, filling it with light.

She waited in the front hall, with its richly waxed floors and oriental runners, where a shining cherry console table sat in front of a gilt-framed mirror. Autumn flowers were arranged beautifully in a silver-and-glass bowl. The hall smelled of furniture polish and flowers and the faint scent of a wood fire in some distant fireplace.

And then her mother appeared, coming down the hall toward her, her bleached blond hair piled on her head in a classic French twist, a string of pearls around her neck. She wore a pale blue silk dress and brown alligator pumps and looked the epitome of the sophisticated West Hartford matron. For a moment, Lindsey wanted to turn and leave the house. She didn't belong here. She'd been a fool to come. Her mother hadn't changed.

But then her mother was extending her hands, her face alight with a smile, her green eyes misted with real tears. "Lindsey, I'm so glad you came. You look wonderful, darling." She took her daughter's hands and squeezed them, looking her up and down, biting on her lower lip, which trembled with emotion. "*God*, Henry would be so *proud* of you!"

At that, Lindsey felt a lump form in her throat. She pulled her hands from her mother's and looked around. "It's quite impressive," she said.

Eliza's smile faltered. "Well..." She shrugged. "Shall we go into the study?"

"The study?" Lindsey said. "That's impressive, too. Sounds so much better than 'the family room.'"

Eliza gave her daughter a shrewd look. "So. It's not going to be easy, is it?"

Lindsey looked away from those knowing eyes. "I guess not."

"Come along, then," Eliza said brightly. "We can still enjoy our tea." She looked at her daughter and added dryly, "I hope."

Lindsey followed her mother down the long hall, glancing at the pictures on the wall, noting the colonial-patterned wallpaper, catching a glimpse of the formal dining room with its twelve-foot-long mahogany table and crystal chandelier.

The study turned out to be a warm and cheerful room, with cherrywood paneling, chintz-covered sofas and armchairs and a fire burning merrily in the fireplace. A golden retriever lolled on the hearth. It lifted its head when Eliza and Lindsey appeared, yawned loudly, then flopped back down and went to sleep.

"That's Rover. Lazy, lazy animal," Eliza said with affectionate disapproval.

A sterling-silver tea set was sitting on the coffee table, with dainty china cups set out next to china plates filled with cookies.

"Well!" said Lindsey when her mother had handed her a cup of tea with honey. "You've done very well for yourself!"

"Did you come here to chastise me?" Eliza asked, arching a patrician brow. "Because if you did, I don't want to hear it. You've done it enough these past ten years."

Lindsey looked away, feeling hot color creep into her cheeks. Now that she was here, she didn't know why she'd come. She couldn't recall the emotions that had seemed so clear in her office. For some reason, she'd thought she needed her mother. How utterly absurd. She'd gone ten years without her. Why would she need her now?

She looked around the beautifully appointed room and felt all her old animosities come flooding back. This is what Eliza had left Henry Andrews for. Well, who could really blame her? It was a lovely room in a beautiful house.

Lindsey sighed and sipped at her tea, and suddenly she was back in the old house, young again. The tea tasted exactly the same as it had then. She stared down at the hand-painted bone-china cup and felt sudden pain twist and tear at her breast. At home there had never been delicate china cups, only heavy chipped ironstone.

"Why did you do it?" she asked brokenly. "Why did you leave Daddy and me?"

Eliza stared at her daughter, her eyes filled with pain. "I didn't love him anymore, Lindsey. But I didn't leave you, darling. I wanted you to come with me, but you refused. You chose to stay with your father. You were eighteen. I felt you were old enough to make up your own mind."

Lindsey raised her head, her eyes cold. "I suppose you were having an affair with Lyman before you even left Daddy."

"No." Eliza looked straight into Lindsey's eyes and shook her head decisively. "I did not have an affair with Lyman while I lived with your father." She lifted her head proudly and Lindsey recognized the gesture with a pang. She used it herself. "Lyman was only a friend then. Our romance developed after I left Henry. I was lonely and afraid and Lyman was good to me. He helped me through the bad times. It happened gradually, but it seemed as if it happened overnight—one day I realized I was in love with him. He asked me to marry him, so I did. I've never regretted it once. Not in ten years."

Cynically, Lindsey glanced around the room. "Well, I don't suppose I'd regret it, either, Mother."

"Yes, you would," her mother said sternly, "if the love died. All the material wealth on earth can't replace love, Lindsey. That's why I left your father. It wasn't the lack of money. It was never that. Money doesn't mean anything. It's love, Lindsey—that's what matters, and Henry and I lost it a good many years before I came to my senses and left him."

Absorbed despite herself, Lindsey stared at her mother. She wasn't just mouthing platitudes, Lindsey realized—she meant everything she'd said. "But I can remember you *shouting* at him!" Lindsey cried. "Always bickering, always belittling him, always telling him he could do better! You never once had a kind word for him. You were a bitch!"

Like the crack of a whip, the word echoed in the quiet room. Eliza's cheeks turned red, as if she'd been slapped. She looked shaken, hurt, but her eyes were filled with a plea for understanding. "If it were a perfect world," she said slowly, "and we were all perfect beings, then perhaps I would have been a perfect wife."

She bent her head and stared down at her fragile hands, which were twisted in her lap. "I'm not proud of how I treated Henry. You're right, of course—I took the wrong tack. I belittled him when I should have stood by him." She sighed and looked out the French windows that overlooked the back garden. "I've always been a strong woman, Lindsey, with no outlet for my ambitions and talents. I didn't go to college. I wasn't trained to be anything but a housewife. And so I lived through the men in my life—a big mistake. At least I did until Lyman taught me that I had executive abilities that could be used in volunteer and charitable organizations.

"But with Henry..." Her voice trailed off, and she looked unbearably sad. "With Henry, I just pushed him and pushed him, hoping he'd succeed for me. I didn't realize that he was a gentle man, with no real ambition to be more than what he was. He stymied me, Lindsey. He frustrated me." She sighed and rubbed her forehead tiredly. "I wasn't a good wife for him. He knew it long before I did, but he was too kind to leave me. He waited until I realized it, then let me go with his blessing."

"His blessing!" Shocked, Lindsey could only stare at her mother.

Smiling sadly, Eliza looked at Lindsey. "You didn't know that, did you? You thought I was the villainess, but your father knew it was right for both of us." She reached into her dress pocket and pulled out a time-worn, creased letter. "I saved this," Eliza said. "When the proper time came, I planned to show it to you. I was hoping today was the proper time."

Lindsey took the fragile letter and opened it. Her heart twisted at the spidery handwriting that she recognized immediately as her father's. She read with tears misting her eyes:

Dearest Eliza:

We've both known for quite some time that our marriage isn't working, which, while being sad, was probably quite inevitable. You are a strong-willed woman, filled with ambition. I'm a quiet man, satisfied with little. We're not at all suited to each other and never have been. That first glorious burst of love we felt for each other was perhaps recognition that we each had something the other lacked. But that doesn't make for a happy life together. You need a stronger man. As for me, I'm not sure I even want another wife. I seem to be a bit monastic. I like the quiet, contemplative life. I will always love you, of course, but it isn't the love a man feels for a wife, rather the love a man feels for a fellow human being. You have my deepest wishes for happiness. Lindsey and I will be fine. You mustn't worry. One day, when Lindsey grows up a little, she'll understand and no longer blame you. She'll see that vows made in ignorance are never meant to be honored.

Love, Henry.

Lindsey stared down at the words, remembering her father's voice as he'd said the same thing to her once long ago. The words swam in front of her, then dissolved into rivers. Her shoulders shook and she wept bitterly, remembering now what had brought her to her mother's home.

"Mama," she said brokenly. "I've missed you so much."

"Oh, Lindsey..." Her mother was beside her in an instant, pulling her into her arms, stroking her hair, holding her close, her eyes squeezed shut despite the tears that escaped from between her wrinkled lids.

"I'm sorry, Mama," Lindsey whispered tearfully. "I'm so very sorry. I've been such a stubborn, willful fool. Please forgive me."

"Lindsey, there's nothing to forgive," Eliza said, smiling through her own tears. "You're here now. That's all that matters."

Lindsey took a deep, shaky breath, then sat back and looked at her mother. "It's good to be here. I'm glad I finally started to grow up."

Her mother smiled widely, then clasped her in a bear hug. "God," she said again, more fervently, "Henry would be so *proud* of you!"

Smiling through her tears, Lindsey returned the hug, sinking into its forgiveness, which she dimly recognized could lead to her salvation.

Eleven

After visiting her mother, Lindsey decided to return to the office and put in some overtime. It seemed strange to wander through deserted corridors that echoed with her solitary footsteps. There was no hustle or bustle, no typewriter keys clicking, no phones ringing, no muffled conversations coming from plushly carpeted offices. She thought she would have the place to herself, but when she arrived, she saw a thin strip of light under Jed's door. Surprised that he was still at work, she headed for his office.

"Hi!" she said, opening his door, then came to a dead stop. He wasn't alone. He wasn't working. A beautiful woman was sitting on his desk, her long, shapely legs crossed as she lit a cigarette from the match Jed cupped in his hand. Her long blond hair trailed over her shoulders, and one four-inch heel dangled seductively off her slender foot.

A second later, the scene dissipated. The woman straightened and swung her hair over her shoulder, staring in surprise at Lindsey. Jed stepped back and extinguished the match. Lindsey just stood and stared, feeling like an oaf who'd just fallen off a pew in the middle of Sunday services.

Then the woman uncrossed and recrossed her spectacular legs and turned to Jed. "A friend of yours?" Her voice was low and a little rough from smoking too many cigarettes. But then that just made her all the sexier.

Lindsey smiled brightly. "Not a friend," she answered. "Just another peon from within the rank and file."

"Oh," the woman said. "She works for you."

"I'm afraid so." The corner of Jed's mouth quirked up as if he thought that amusing. Lindsey gave him a pointed glance and turned to go to her office. "Sorry I disturbed you. I might have known you wouldn't be working." With that she tossed her head and slammed her door shut.

Gritting her teeth, she swore colorfully under her breath and wondered why she'd had to break in on that particular scene. It only confirmed her view of Jed—he'd wine and dine any attractive woman and wasn't to be trusted in the least. If she had ever entertained the possibility of falling in love with him, that colorful little scenario should wipe out the thought forever.

But for some reason it didn't. It made things worse. Lindsey sat at her desk and tried to concentrate on a report, but she kept finding herself staring into space, frowning, tapping her pen in agitation as she remembered the woman, whom Jed hadn't even bothered to introduce.

So that was the kind he liked—sexy, sophisticated, slender to the point of being gaunt. She'd had rather a hard face and Lindsey hated her as much now as she had at first sight. Which was illogical, of course. The kind of woman Jed Wentworth dated shouldn't have any effect on her, but for some reason it did. Lindsey went around in circles, spitting mad at the memory of the intimate scene she'd stumbled upon, even as she told herself it was none of her business.

She was grinding her teeth in frustration when her office door opened and Jed appeared. "Hi."

Looking up, she said, "Sorry there's no one here for you to stumble on."

"You didn't come back to meet Peter Gibson for a late-night assignation?"

"Afraid not," Lindsey said brightly, indicating the papers scattered all over her desk. "I'm here to work." She smiled sweetly. "Unlike you."

"Why the sudden conscientiousness? Have you been slacking off during the day?"

"I never slack off."

"Maybe you should." Jed sat down and put his feet up on her desk. "Noses pressed to the grindstone all the time aren't very sexy."

She glanced pointedly at his feet invading her personal space, but decided not to make an issue of it. "I wasn't aware sexiness was a requirement for an assistant to the president of a company," Lindsey said dryly. She laughed. "But then I am naive, aren't I?"

"Very," he agreed affably. "Have you eaten dinner yet?"

"No." She made a point of studying the report in front of her. Maybe he'd take the hint and leave.

"I haven't, either. Let's go out and get something."

She stopped writing in midsentence, then forced herself to go on as if nothing unusual had been said. "Sorry, I need to finish this report."

"You little coward," he said softly. "You're going to fink out on me, aren't you? You're trying to make up an excuse not to go out with me."

She ignored him and continued to scribble nonsense on the pad of paper, praying he wouldn't look at it, because if he did he'd immediately see her for the fraud she was.

"Well?" Jed prodded.

"Well what?"

"Will you go out to dinner with me?"

"What's wrong with Tootsie?" Lindsey asked sarcastically. "Didn't she have time for dinner with you?"

"Tootsie?"

"The doll in your office."

"Oh, Anne," he said casually. "No, she just stopped by for a chat."

"Uh-huh."

"You sound jealous."

"Why would I be jealous?" Lindsey said. "Your personal life is your affair, not mine."

"No, but it could be," Jed said.

Sighing in exasperation, Lindsey gave him a look and went back to scribbling. "Thanks for the invitation," she said finally, "but I've got lots of things to do and I thought I'd catch up on them tonight."

"You'd rather work overtime than go out to dinner with me?"

She put down her pen and met his amused gaze. "It does seem odd, doesn't it, that a perfectly sane woman would prefer to work than go out with you, but there you have it." Shrugging, she picked up her pen again. "Good night, Jed. Nice talking with you."

He tipped his chair back and balanced neatly on two legs as he studied her. "You disappoint me, Lindsey, you really do."

"Do I?" she said, continuing to scribble. "What a shame."

"You don't sound very repentant."

"Probably because I'm not."

Jed sighed and tipped his chair down. "I can see I'm going to have to exercise a little power here. It's a shame, but..." He stood up and put his hands on her desk and leaned toward her. "Put down that damn pen and come to dinner with me," he ordered.

She looked up at him. "No."

"Careful, Lindsey, this is your boss speaking."

"The answer is still no."

"I have big news."

"What is it?"

"Uh-uh. No way. You have to come to dinner with me. Or wait to read it in tomorrow's paper. My visitor was Anne Rutledge, the business reporter from the *Sentinel*. She's going to break some news in a story tomorrow." He straightened and shoved his hands into his pockets and began strolling around Lindsey's office. "Of course if you want to be in the dark and read about it in the papers like everyone else, then that's your problem. It won't look good, of course, for my very own personal assistant not to know what's going on, but again, that's your problem."

"You're blackmailing me," she cried.

"Uh-huh." He looked back at her. "Coming?"

She struggled with her frustration and finally threw down her pen. "What's the big deal about my having dinner with you? You just have to prove you can get me to go out with you, don't you? That ego of yours is incredible. You just can't take defeat, can you? You've got to win."

"Exactly," he said, straightening his tie. "Where do you want to go?"

"Why do you do this?" she asked. "What's the big deal about getting your way?"

"Humor me, Lindsey. I'm male. My ego needs stroking every now and then. Just come to dinner and stop putting up such a fuss."

"Anne must have really put you down," she said dryly.

"Actually, she invited me to dinner at her place tonight but I refused." He smiled. "Coming?"

"I hate this," Lindsey said. "I hate this game-playing, these power moves. It is just so incredibly frustrating."

"Lindsey, shut up and get your things. I'm hungry."

"Precisely," she said bitterly. "*You're* hungry, so little Lindsey has to heel."

Jed turned back from the door and studied her thoughtfully. "I'm sorry. That *was* crude of me. *Please* shut up and get your things."

"Ohhhhhhh!" she groaned.

Grinning amiably, Jed held the door for her. "That's what I like about you, Lindsey. You're just so accommodating. You make a man feel so important. You flatter me so much, fawn, bow and scrape, and grovel. You'll do just about anything to please me, won't you?"

"Jed," she said, staring straight ahead as they waited for the elevator. "Just shut up."

Grinning, he took her arm and escorted her into the elevator.

"How did Peter manage to get the Governor to agree to come to the ground-breaking?" Lindsey asked between forkfuls of linguine with clam sauce. "That's really a coup."

Jed shrugged and twirled his spaghetti around his fork. "Gibson's a smooth talker. That's why I hired him—" He darted an amused look at Lindsey. "No offense to present company, of course."

"None taken."

"I wouldn't be surprised if Gibson resigns the minute the river project is done. He's ambitious. I can see him wanting to be a governmental spokesman someday. If he gets in with the Governor now, maybe a few years down the road he'll be offered a job as his press secretary. Five years later,

I can see him in Washington, press secretary to the President."

"Well, his ego is certainly big enough for the job," said Lindsey emphatically.

"You sound as if you've brushed up against it."

"That visit he paid me at my place was none too friendly, although I think he wanted it to be—ergo, the champagne. But it soon deteriorated when he found out I wasn't drinking, so to speak." Lindsey shook her head. "Nope, I wouldn't want to cross swords with Peter every day. I happened to get lucky today, but I wouldn't bet on my chances most of the time."

"He bought your memo then, short and succinct as it was?"

"He bought it. I got to talking about Connecticut and everything that makes it so special and he picked up on what I couldn't put into words on paper. He realized he has to come up with something more than just a polished brochure. Image is so ephemeral, it's hard to even talk about it, but he got the picture quickly. I really think he'll bring in something good the next time."

"I'm glad you agree with my choice for Director of Advertising and Publicity then."

"I do—reluctantly, of course. I realize now that while I may have the love for and knowledge of Connecticut, I don't have the professionalism and polish that Peter has."

"That's why I thought you'd make a good team," Jed said. "You complement each other. But I didn't want you actually working for him, I wanted you with me. I think we make a great team, too."

Lindsey eyed Jed uneasily. They had somehow agreed to make peace for the evening and, to her surprise, she was enjoying herself. That still didn't mean she should trust him, of course. Only a fool would trust Jed Wentworth. Then she found herself wondering if she was right. Sometimes she got the feeling Jed wasn't the womanizer she thought he was.

"We do okay," she admitted, swirling her fork in her uneaten linguine. She looked up and met Jed's gaze. "I'm glad you suggested dinner tonight. It *is* nice just to be able to sit and talk with you, instead of feeling I have to be constantly on guard against you."

"You've never had to be, Lindsey," Jed said. "I'd never try to take advantage of you, or push myself on you. What happened last night was—" Frowning, he shook his head, as if he couldn't explain himself adequately. "I guess I just overreacted. I show up on your doorstep and find you looking deliciously seductive, with Peter Gibson and a bottle of champagne. I'm sorry. I was way out of line. I won't let it happen again."

"If I won't get involved with you, Jed, why would you think I'd get involved with Peter?"

"He's not your boss, for one thing. You work in different departments, on different floors. And he's very attractive."

"He's not all that attractive," Lindsey said offhandedly.

"No?"

She glanced at Jed and smiled. "I find dark men more appealing, if you must know."

"Why does that knowledge make my heart beat a little faster?" Jed asked, smiling.

She returned his smile automatically, before she could stop herself. It was comfortable being here with him in this cozy Italian restaurant in Hartford's south end. Just for tonight, she decided, she could let her guard down a little and enjoy his company. Tomorrow she could go back to being the Human Machine with no heart and no feelings, but tonight she'd enjoy herself. Remembering her realization from earlier that day and the special conversation with her mother, she felt a shadow cross her face. Maybe she had needed this night out with Jed. Maybe she'd kept too tight a lid on her personal life the past couple years....

"Something wrong?" Jed asked.

"No." Lindsey hesitated. "Why did you ask?"

"Your face changed. You looked almost sad. Any special reason?"

Lindsey toyed with her food. "No," she said, then shrugged. "Well, maybe a little special." Suddenly uncomfortable, she pushed her wineglass away. She didn't know how much she could tell Jed about her relationship with her mother, but she certainly knew she didn't want to talk about her father. "I went to see my mother today."

"What made that so special?"

"Well, I guess the fact that I haven't visited with her for ten years might make it special," she said airily, hoping that her vulnerability didn't show too much.

"Ten *years*?"

Lindsey smiled uneasily. "Kind of a long time, huh?" She rubbed her forehead worriedly. "It's hard to talk about."

"I see..." Jed swirled his wine in his glass, peering at it then at Lindsey. He poured more into her glass but didn't say anything.

Lindsey cradled her glass in her hands, staring over its rim into the past. Suddenly she felt like talking: "My mother left my father ten years ago," she said slowly. "It was very difficult for me. I felt as if she were betraying him when she walked out. I decided to stay with him and cut all ties with Mother. I'd see her every once in a while of course. One couldn't help it. Mother's on every charity board in the Hartford area. And you know she's married to Lyman Cartwright, and so inevitably I'd be at social functions and we'd meet. And she'd call every once in a while, trying to break through to me, I guess."

"It appears she finally managed to," Jed said. When Lindsey looked puzzled, he explained: "You went to visit her today."

"Yes. Well!" She paused, still feeling uncomfortable with the subject. "Let's not talk about it anymore."

"Fine," Jed said agreeably. "If that's how you really feel."

"Why wouldn't it be?" Lindsey asked.

"I get the feeling you need to talk with someone, that's all."

Lindsey stared into her wine, then lifted her eyes to Jed. She did need to talk with someone—to share and communicate and open up, but why with Jed? Why was he the one who was drawing her out? She couldn't understand it, but she knew it felt right. Suddenly it felt as if the floodgates had opened. "I've begun to question some of my priorities, I guess," she said. "And to wonder just how important making it as a career woman really is." She shook her head, wondering what she was saying. "Well, of course it's very important, but I've also begun to think that other things are important too. People, for instance. Specifically, my mother."

Jed rested his chin in his hand. "Good. Now if you'd just open your eyes and look across the table, you'd see someone else you might begin caring about."

Startled, Lindsey stared at him, then laughed. "Will you stop? Can't you ever be serious? Do you always have to flirt? It's like some congenital defect with you."

"Who said I was flirting?" he asked mildly.

"Oh, come *on*, Jed!"

He studied her thoughtfully, then looked away. "Oh, well, I guess you're right. It's a habit, I suppose."

Frowning, she stared at him. Something seemed funny—funny strange. For just a moment, it almost appeared that Jed *had* been serious. She shifted in her chair and wondered what was going on. Were her instincts as good as she thought they were, or was it possible she'd been wrong about Jed?

"So tell me more about this priority-shifting stuff," Jed said, pouring more wine. "It's interesting—like listening to a geologist talk about the San Andreas fault."

She smiled despite herself. "I've compartmentalized my life, as if one part is Church and the other is State. I began to see that my life's been pretty sterile the past couple years." She looked down, feeling embarrassed at her revelations. "I've needed someone to talk to like this," she admitted softly. "You don't know how precious it is, just to have someone to talk to."

"Don't I?" Jed swirled the wine in his glass again. "Do you think it's any easier for me, Lindsey? You think a man who works as long and hard as I do has any more time for friends than you do? Don't get me wrong—I love my work. It's food for my soul. But it does get lonely at the top.

"A few years ago there was a woman I was very attracted to, but she couldn't share my enthusiasm for new buildings. She'd yawn whenever I talked business, and as you know, I talk business quite a lot." He sighed tiredly. "I've begun to wonder if a man has to live two lives—the one at work that feeds his soul, and the one at home that feeds his physical needs. More than anything, I've been looking for a woman who can share everything with me, not just a bed."

Lindsey stared at him. Was this the Jed Wentworth she thought she knew, the man who seduced women, then discarded them like old packs of cigarettes? She was struck yet again with the realization that she had a terrible failing—she made automatic assumptions about people that weren't always borne out by reality. She'd done it with her parents, and now she began to suspect she'd been doing it with Jed.

She felt ashamed, as if she'd judged a defendant before any evidence had been presented.

"I hope you find her someday, Jed," she said softly, filled with remorse.

He looked at Lindsey oddly and said, "Yes, so do I." Then he grinned. "Of course, in the meantime, I'm open to a little hanky-panky with my administrative assistant."

Lindsey shook her head. He was incorrigible. "Jed, if there's one thing a woman who wants a career learns, it's not to get involved with someone at work. But an even bigger problem is getting involved with her boss. It leaves a woman open to all kinds of accusations—that's she's promoted because of their relationship, or she's been given perks out of favoritism. It just doesn't work. The woman always loses in the end. The scandal alone can ruin her reputation. If she's serious about a career, that's like heading a ship toward rocks in a hurricane."

"That's supposing that things don't work out between the man and woman. But what if they do? What if they fall deeply in love? What if they want to get married? What if they want to share not only their work but their personal lives as well?"

"The odds are against it."

"The hell with the odds," Jed said angrily. "We'd make our own odds."

Startled, Lindsey stared at him. They had suddenly gone from discussing the general to the specific—her and Jed—and again she got the strong impression he was serious. What was going on? She laughed, troubled by the double messages she seemed to be getting. "Better be careful, Mr. Wentworth, a woman just might take you seriously one of these days."

He tilted his head consideringly. "And what would be so bad about that?"

Lindsey laughed again. "Everything! It would be a disaster! No woman in her right mind should ever take you seriously."

Jed sighed and poured more wine. "Great. And here I thought this little romantic dinner would do the trick and you'd fall into my arms and let me make mad, passionate love to you tonight."

Lindsey looked down quickly to hide the sudden awareness that flowered within her. The thought of making love with Jed was utterly intoxicating. She felt a little dizzy just imagining it. But maybe it was the wine. It had to be the wine. Any other explanation was just too frightening.

"I think it's time for me to go home," she said.

Jed sighed. "I'm striking out again, I take it."

"Sorry," she said. "Maybe next time."

"I'll hold you to that, Lindsey."

Smiling, she rose from the table. "Good night, Mr. Wentworth. Thank you for a lovely evening. Even if it did start out as blackmail."

"But aren't you glad you know about the groundbreaking ceremonies before it's in the paper tomorrow?"

"Very glad," she said. "Good night, Jed."

"Good night, Lindsey."

She left him sitting at the table, pouring himself more wine.

Twelve

That night, when Lindsey got in bed, she found herself unable to sleep. Instead, she began to imagine what it would be like to make love with Jed Wentworth. She saw it all, watching in fascination as Jed unbuttoned her blouse, caressed her breasts, slowly eased his hand between her legs. In her vivid imagination, he did everything a man could do to a woman, with expertise such as she'd never experienced. His tongue invaded her, his fingers lightly brushed over her skin, titillating her, inciting her to more ardent desire.

She grew restive, turning languidly in her bed, wishing he was there, wishing she was naked in his arms. Her fantasies grew more graphic until finally she had to get out of bed and pace the floor, her arms folded tightly around herself as if warding off a chill. She knotted her hand into a fist and thrust it against her mouth and bit down on it, hard, holding back a groan of pure frustration.

Finally she threw on her robe and stomped downstairs. There was only one way to get through the night, and that was to work. She pulled some papers from her briefcase and began reading. Two hours later, she was finally calm enough to climb the stairs and retire safely to her bed.

"Sleep well last night?" Jed asked cheerfully the next morning.

Lindsey pasted a wide grin on her face and nodded energetically. "Great! You?"

Jed stretched lazily, looking as satisfied as the cat who lapped up the cream. "Terrific," he said. "Just terrific."

Lindsey's face fell. "Oh." She forced a smile. "How nice."

"Yes, it was. We'll have to go out for dinner again sometime. I could use a couple more early nights like that once in a while."

Lindsey stared at him, then turned on her heel and walked into her office. Seconds later, Jed was beside her.

"Anything the matter, Lindsey?"

"Nothing at all," she said, ordering herself to sound cheerful. "Why do you ask?"

"I don't know. I suppose the way you walked out of my office without replying worried me."

She kept her head down as she shuffled through her papers. "No need to be worried, Jed. I guess I've got this report on my mind."

"It's always work with you, isn't it?"

"That's what you pay me for."

"Did you see the article in the *Sentinel* about the groundbreaking?"

"Actually, I didn't," she said. She'd been thinking so much about Jed and how attracted she was to him that she'd forgotten all about the riverfront project. The realization was a blow to her. She stared at Jed, then looked away uneasily, hoping he couldn't read her like a book.

He shrugged, shoving his hands into his trouser pockets and rocking back on his heels. "You might want to read it sometime. It's a nice article."

"All right," she said. "Now do you have anything else to say? I really *am* busy, Jed." She went back to shuffling through her papers, pretending to be searching for something.

"What are you looking for? Maybe I can help."

"No!" she said, then smiled quickly to hide her dismay. "That's nice of you, but you wouldn't have the least idea where to look."

"I would if you'd tell me."

Lindsey broke off looking through her papers and lifted exasperated eyes to his. "Jed, I slept miserably last night. Now please just leave me alone."

"But that's just the trouble, Lindsey," Jed said softly. "I did leave you alone last night, and look what happened. You got all mean and ornery on me."

"I—" She stared at him, afraid to speak. She didn't know what to say, suddenly couldn't even think. All she could see was Jed standing close enough to touch, and all she could remember were the fantasies that had kept her awake last night.

He rested a muscular thigh on the corner of her desk. "I think I'd better stay and help you out. You seem a little frazzled. And you're beginning to forget things. When you first came in, you said you slept great." He smiled at her genially. "Did you or didn't you?"

"Did I or didn't I what?" she asked woodenly.

"Sleep well?"

She took a tremulous breath and tried to push the thoughts of why she hadn't slept out of her mind. "How I slept is none of your business," she said, going back to shuffling her papers. At least this way she felt a semblance of control.

"If you'd slept with me, you would have slept great," he said easily, then seemed to have second thoughts: "But, then again..." He broke into a huge grin. His blue eyes were twinkling devilishly. She felt a spasm of awareness in her stomach and had to take a deep breath to steady herself.

"Jed, just go away."

"But I don't want to go away, Lindsey. I've been letting you set the tempo long enough. Now we're going to play things my way."

"Jed—" she began, then was swept headlong into his arms and she couldn't say another word. He was kissing her and she was responding and she couldn't stop herself. It was what she wanted more than anything, what had kept her awake half the night, what her entire body seemed made for. Giving in to the ecstasy, she put her arms around his neck and melted into his embrace, parting her lips to allow the kisses to deepen. She began to grow dizzy, but it was a delicious dizziness, such as she'd never experienced before. She felt as if she were whirling and twirling in a magnificent waltz. Dimly, she could even hear music playing—the soaring strings of thousands of violins, the trill of harps, the singing of angels.

"Oh, Jed," she said, breaking away. "We can't do this."

"But we just did," he murmured, running a hand through her hair. "And it felt good. I think we should do it some more." He drew her into his embrace again but this time she tried to fight it.

"No, I don't think this is a good idea."

"I think it's a great idea and I'm the boss, remember?"

"Stop it! You make everything sound so simple, and it isn't."

"That's where you're wrong. You're the one who's making everything difficult. Just kiss me, Lindsey, and everything will begin to fall into place."

"What if Margaret walked in? Or Peter Gibson? How would it look?"

"Who cares how it would look?"

"*I* care! It's not your job on the line. It's not your reputation that would be shattered, it's mine." She stared at him, so frustrated she couldn't see straight. "Jed, listen to me! I can't get involved with you. I just *can't*."

"Yet last night you indicated you were beginning to wonder if a career was everything in life. Well, I'm offering you the chance to have both—a job with me and a relationship with me."

"Jed, it's not that simple...."

"Let me show you how simple it is," he murmured, and pulled her into his arms again.

She tried to resist but couldn't, and finally went willingly into the safe harbor he offered, clinging to him, letting her arms go up and around his neck, holding on to him as if he were a rock and she was lost in stormy seas.

"You feel so wonderful," Jed murmured against her neck. "I could hold you like this forever."

"I wish you could," Lindsey whispered, her eyes closed as she savored the way his lips caressed her. "Oh, I wanted you so much last night," she whispered. "I thought I'd die from wanting you."

"It's about time you finally admitted it," he said, drawing her even closer, letting his lips travel over her face, dropping light kisses on her closed lids, her brow, her cheeks, her ear.

She opened her eyes and searched his face. Was he toying with her, or did he truly care about her? "I had one relationship with a man who just wanted sex," she said finally. "I don't want another, Jed. I want it all—the physical and the emotional fulfillment of real love. Can you offer me that?"

He hesitated, then said, "I guess we'll just have to take the chance and find out."

"I've never been much of a risk-taker, Jed," she said. "If I got involved with you, it would be the biggest risk of my life."

"If I'm willing to risk it, why aren't you?"

"Jed, you don't have anything to lose. You're president of this corporation. You won't lose your job if things don't work out—"

"Neither would you," he said heatedly. "Dammit, Lindsey, I'd never fire you if things didn't work out. I'm not made that way."

"What would you do, then? Offer me a job in the file room?"

He stared at her, a muscle working agitatedly in his jaw. "Lindsey, I want you, and I know by the way you respond to me you want me, too. I've stood by the past two months and let you set the pace, but dammit, it's a *turtle's* pace! I'm not going to let you push me away much longer."

"So you want me and I'm supposed to fall into your arms, is that it?" she asked, her voice as heated as his. "I'm sorry, Mr. Wentworth, but it doesn't always work that way. This woman's not playing by your rules. She makes up her own."

"You make it sound as if it's just a game."

"Isn't it?" she challenged.

He stared at her. "I'm not offering you a one-night stand if that's what you're afraid of."

"Oh? How many nights would it be, then? Two? Three? Five or six with a weekend trip to Atlantic City thrown in for added spice?"

"I'm offering you a chance at something real and something solid, but if you're too afraid to take a chance then maybe you're not the woman I think you are."

She stared at him, afraid to believe what he was saying. He was giving her an ultimatum, but she couldn't respond to it. She needed time. All this was happening much too quickly. Suddenly everything was too confusing. Her world had been turned topsy-turvy and she didn't know which way was up.

"I can't take any chances yet, Jed. Not now, not with you."

He sighed and shoved his hand through his hair. "Looks like I'll just have to keep coming after you, then." He smiled lopsidedly and turned to leave. At the door, he looked back. "Have a nice day, Lindsey. And by the way, I came in here earlier, before you got to work, and had a look at that report you were so busy working on last night."

Aghast, Lindsey felt her face drain of all color. "Oh?" she asked in a strangled voice. She couldn't remember what she'd written last night when she'd scribbled on the pad, but she knew it had been garbage. "What did you think of it?" she asked brightly.

"I think that part you were working on last night needs a little revision. Maybe we could get together later and work on it." Quietly, he shut the door.

Lindsey stood a moment, then tore over to her desk and shuffled through the pages. When she found the final page, she read it and felt her face grow crimson. Last night, she'd thought she was just scribbling, but she saw now she hadn't been. The words were garbled, but anyone with half a brain could decipher the meaning. She'd written the words "Jed and Bed," and "Love or Sex?" over and over, all the way down the page.

At the end, in Jed's neat handwriting, was a short note: "Most of the report is fine, but this last part is really intriguing. Maybe we should get together and discuss it. Let's have dinner again tonight and see where things go from there."

Mortified, she sank into her chair and put her head in her hands. Dear heavens, things were getting murkier and murkier. *Now* what was she going to do...?

Margaret Oliver strode briskly into Lindsey's office a little after four. "Mr. Wentworth asked me to tell you he'll meet you tonight at seven at El Dorado."

"Tonight at—" Astounded, Lindsey stared at Margaret.

"Seven," Margaret promptly responded. "Seven precisely, Ms. Andrews. You know he doesn't like people who are late." She brushed off a speck of lint and said self-importantly, "I've worked for him for fifteen years and have never been late a day. Not once, Ms. Andrews." Margaret nodded decisively. "So. That's that. He'll meet you at El Dorado at seven." She turned to go, then hesitated. "I suppose you'll go," she said with obvious disapproval.

Lindsey lifted her hands helplessly. "What else can I do? It sounds as if I've been given a royal summons."

Margaret eyed Lindsey knowingly. "It wouldn't be smart to sleep with him, Ms. Andrews. Not smart at all." Margaret's eyes narrowed. "Or have you already?"

Lindsey's face reddened. "I beg your pardon?" she said, offended and showing it. "What are you talking about?"

"Oh, come off it, Ms. Andrews—it's very obvious Mr. Wentworth is attracted to you, but you'd be a fool to sleep with him." She shook her head severely. "Take it from me. *I* know."

"Oh?" Lindsey asked coldly. "Have you already slept with him?"

Affronted, Margaret bristled. "Don't be silly! I'm old enough to be his mother, but he's not the *only* man I've worked for..."

Suddenly things fell into place and Margaret made sense. At some point in her life, when she was younger, she'd had an affair with her boss that had turned out disastrously. It had obviously soured her for life. Stricken with compassion, Lindsey's face grew tender. "I'm sorry, Margaret," she said softly. "It sounds as if you do know what you're talking about."

That seemed to be the only opening Margaret needed. She drew up a chair, then looked hesitantly at Lindsey. "May I?"

"Of course."

Relieved, Margaret sat down, then looked around uncomfortably. "I know you think I'm an old Scrooge," she said at last. "And I suppose most of the time I am." Her hands grappled with each other nervously in her lap. "But I can see what's going on between you two and—" She hesitated and her hardened face crumpled. Suddenly she was no longer the vigilant old curmudgeon who patrolled Jed's outer office. She was an elderly woman, alone and lonely, looking terribly vulnerable.

"Go on, Margaret," Lindsey said quietly.

"I know it's none of my business," Margaret said worriedly. "And I know Jed's a fine man. In all the years I've worked for him, he's never gotten involved with anyone who works for him. That's why he hired me. He told me he wanted an old battle-ax in the office so he wouldn't be tempted to pinch my behind." Margaret laughed at the memory, then glanced nervously at Lindsey.

"He was joking, of course. As I said, he's never once been involved with anyone who works here. But then you came along and I could see right away you were different. He lights up when you're around. He watches you when you're not looking." Margaret smiled gently. "He gets this look on his face," she said tenderly. "The most beautiful look, as if he truly *cares* for you—"

She broke off, clearly troubled. "But I can't help worrying," she continued, "because I got involved with my first boss years ago. Oh, it was foolish of me. He was married and I should have known better, but he was so good-looking I couldn't resist the man. He'd close that office door and I was a goner." She twisted her hands in her lap. "I'd just hate to see that happen to you, Ms. Andrews. You've always been sweet to me, even when I'm rotten to you. I don't *mean* to be rotten. It's just..." Margaret glanced downward. "I got bitter, I guess. I fell in love with my boss and he used me for years. I thought he'd leave his wife and marry me, but when *his* boss found out about us, I was fired and he forgot all about me. It was over just like that." She snapped her fingers, then sighed tiredly. "I'm sorry, I have no right to butt in like this."

"I'm glad you told me, Margaret," Lindsey said softly. "I've always wondered why—well, why you aren't too friendly. Now I understand."

Margaret straightened her thin shoulders and seemed to pull herself together. "Yes. Well!" She raised her chin and looked old, but undefeated. "I may be an old harridan, but that doesn't mean I don't see things. I'm just warning you to be careful, Lindsey. Mr. Wentworth seems to care for you, but you're in a difficult position. It never pays to get involved with one's boss. Take it from an expert."

"I know that, Margaret," Lindsey said. "But I still appreciate your concern." She hesitated, then said slowly, "I haven't slept with him, you know, but you are right, there is a...how shall I say it? There's an attraction between us."

"Well, any fool can see that!" Margaret said explosively, then sat back. "There I go again," she fretted. "Being obnoxious."

Lindsey smiled. "You're not so obnoxious. Now that you're talking with me, I kind of like you, Margaret."

"You do?" Margaret looked up, clearly surprised, but also clearly pleased. She suddenly looked happier, more hopeful, as if she'd walked outside expecting to find rain and had found bright sunshine instead. "Well, I must say, I rather like you, too, Ms. Andrews—er, Lindsey."

"Thank you for the warning, Margaret. It isn't easy being a working woman, is it? I guess it was even harder twenty or thirty years ago."

"Yes, it was," Margaret agreed. "And it's still hard. We're women, so we have these soft hearts, and we meet these wonderful men and can't help falling in love, but—" she shook her head, her eyes worried "—it's not simple, is it? Men don't have to worry about all this. There's that damn double standard that protects them. If they get caught philandering with the secretary, they're given a rap on the hand by the boss and then they get together and laugh about it later in the bar over drinks. But with women..." She shook her head again. "We can't let our guard drop for a minute, because if we do, we could lose everything—our hearts *and* our jobs."

"So what's the answer, Margaret?" Lindsey asked sadly. "Would you have done things differently now that you know what can happen?"

Margaret hesitated. "That's a difficult question, Lindsey, more difficult than you can know. I really loved that man. I loved him with all my heart and soul. For me, it didn't work out. But who's to say it can't? Should we give up a chance at love and become nothing more than unfeeling machines at work?" She sighed and shook her head. "I can't answer that one. All I know is, when I worked with Eugene I glowed." Margaret Oliver smiled softly as she remembered the past. "I'm not really sure I'd want to give that up, even if it didn't work out for me. I had it once, you see—I had the golden ring. For a few brief, shining years, I was in love. Perhaps that's what makes life worthwhile, Lindsey—taking the chance, even though you might lose."

Thirteen

Margaret's words haunted Lindsey for the next couple of hours. She sat at her desk and stared sightlessly into the future, trying to discern what might happen. It was impossible, of course, as fruitless as hoping you'd win the lottery when you didn't even have the money to buy a ticket. She wondered if she should simply go home and forget about meeting Jed at El Dorado, but something kept her from doing that. Perhaps she was simply a fool, but she was drawn to Jed as a dieter is drawn to food. All the common sense in the world and all the determination to do what was right seemed small comfort when one was confronted with the possibility of taking a chance on love.

She thought of Margaret and what had happened to her, and rebellion at the sheer injustice of a woman's lot in life rose up within her. Yet she knew that anger at the way the world worked wouldn't help her now. The deck was stacked against her and she had to accept that. Jed owned Wentworth Enterprises. He was lord and master here. If she got involved with him, he wouldn't be the one who suffered. While she knew that, Jed couldn't seem to comprehend it. Never having been a woman, he couldn't summon the necessary empathy to understand why Lindsey was so afraid to get involved with him. It all came back to that seemingly unbridgeable gap between males and females, she thought desolately. Men and women were as different as oil and water. There seemed to be no common ground from which they could look at the world, no shared experiences from which to build a common perspective.

At a quarter to seven, Lindsey put on her jacket and turned out the lights and made her way to the El Dorado restaurant. When she asked to be shown to the table Jed had reserved, the maître d' said, "Ah yes, Ms. Andrews. There is a limousine outside waiting for you."

"A limousine?"

"Mr. Wentworth has changed his plans, Ms. Andrews. He's asked us to please see that you are escorted safely to the car, which will take you to his home."

"I see..." Suddenly everything seemed vibrantly clear. Jed wanted to get her alone so he could turn up the thermostat on their already sizzling attraction to one another. He'd probably woo her with champagne and soft music. He'd tease and flirt and dazzle her with attention. He probably assumed she'd become like putty in his hands. A slow smile flickered at the corner of her lips, then died. "All right," she said quietly. "Where is the car?"

A man escorted her to the sleek black limousine and saw her inside. Then the car glided smoothly away. Lindsey sank back in the plush seats, feeling her heart begin to drum in her breast. She was playing with fire and she knew it, yet she couldn't seem to stop herself. It would have been wiser to have turned around and walked out of El Dorado and gone home, but some demon had kept her from doing that. She'd told herself she was going to Jed's home to put him in his place once and for all, but another part of her acknowledged that she wanted to be with Jed, wanted to be seduced. She was tired of being watchful, tired of denying herself what she had desired for so long.

At last the limousine came to a stop outside the impressive front entrance of a huge mansion on a hilltop in Bloomfield. The door of the limousine was opened by the driver and Lindsey stepped out. She could still change her mind and demand that he take her back to El Dorado and her car, but she knew that was the coward's way out. Lindsey raised her chin and set her mouth in a firm line and let herself be led to the majestic front doors of Jed's estate.

An elderly man opened the door, thanked the driver for his help, then escorted Lindsey across a mammoth foyer to an even larger room where a fire crackled cheerfully in the grate and sherry waited on the cocktail table in Waterford decanters. Subdued white-linen-covered couches were heaped with rust-colored needlepoint pillows. An Oriental carpet covered the polished parquet floor. Priceless Chinese vases ornamented antique desks, and fresh flowers decorated the room, filling it with their sweet scent.

"Sherry, Ms. Andrews?" the elderly gentleman asked.

"No, thank you," she said, summoning a brief smile for him.

"Mr. Wentworth will be right with you, ma'am. He asked me to make you comfortable and see that you have anything you might need."

"I'm fine, thank you," Lindsey said, and smiled again. The old man nodded and disappeared from the room.

Lindsey sat down on one of the couches and crossed her legs, looking around the impressive room, wondering what to expect when Jed appeared. Would he try to seduce her, and, even more important, would she let him?

"Are you angry?" Jed asked from the doorway behind her.

Her heart lurched but she pretended to be in control. "No. Should I be?"

He strolled around the couch and stood looking down at her. "I wasn't sure how you'd take the change of plans."

She shrugged. "How should I take them, Jed?"

"You're playing it very cool."

She smiled. "Just waiting to see exactly what the game is."

"It's not a game, Lindsey. I just wanted you to come to dinner at my home, that's all."

She studied him, then shook her head, smiling ruefully. "You decided you'd get me here alone and seduce me, you mean."

"I knew you'd say that!" Jed said. "I knew it!"

"Then why'd you even bother?" Lindsey asked. "Honestly, Jed, you are utterly transparent. Why didn't you just walk into my office and suggest we go to a motel?"

"Because I don't want to go to a motel with you," Jed said. "I wanted to have dinner with you at my home. I knew you'd never come if I simply invited you, so I resorted to subterfuge. I'm sorry, Lindsey."

"About as sorry as a bear who stumbles on a jar of honey," she said, unable to keep the bitterness out of her voice.

"Lindsey, promptly at midnight my driver will reappear and take you home. He'll arrange to have your car returned to your home, or, if you prefer, he'll drive you back to El Dorado where you can drive your own car home. It's your choice. I have no intention of keeping you here tonight, of seducing you or even touching you. In fact, I'll stay halfway across the room all night if that will make you feel more comfortable."

"Then why am I here?"

"For dinner," he said softly. "You're here for dinner."

She searched his eyes, wondering if she would ever be able to believe Jed Wentworth. Finally she asked, "You couldn't have just asked me to come to dinner?"

"Would you have believed that's all I wanted?"

"No," she admitted reluctantly.

"Well, then, there you have it. A quandary, for both of us. I solved it in the only way I knew how."

"It was underhanded."

"Honesty wouldn't have worked."

"It smacks of a power play."

He shrugged. "What's the use of having power if you don't use it once in a while?"

"Are you sure I'm not meant to be dessert?"

He sighed and poured himself some sherry. "Dessert is apple pie. I know it's not very exciting, but it's what I like—good, simple, down-home American food." He glanced at her. "I can call my driver back. There's a phone in the car. He'll take you back to El Dorado now if you like."

Lindsey didn't respond right away. She struggled over her decision, not knowing what to do. "I'll stay," she said at last.

"Don't let me put you out," he said ironically.

She looked away, ashamed that she'd attributed ulterior motives to him, yet still afraid to trust him. "I'm sorry," she said in a low voice. "It appears I owe you an apology."

"None necessary," Jed said, taking a seat on the opposite end of the couch. "What do you think of the Mets' chances of going to the Series?"

She laughed with relief to be on such a neutral topic. "I haven't been watching them all that much lately," she replied. "But they'll win the eastern division. I'm sure of that."

"We could watch them for a while before dinner," Jed suggested.

"Yes," she said slowly, "I suppose we could."

Grinning, he reached for a remote-control device. A large TV screen glided down from the ceiling, then, as if by magic, the Mets appeared on it. Gooden was on the mound.

Jed put his feet up and rested his head against the couch cushions. "I've dreamed about this, Lindsey," he said after a few moments.

Lindsey wasn't sure what he meant. "About what?" she asked finally.

"About you being here with me, watching television, sharing a meal, just being here."

She looked away, dazed. A shiver went through her, then, unaccountably, she felt tears well up in her eyes. For the first time, she believed him. There was something so sincere in his voice that she could no longer doubt him. Quietly, she got up and went and sat beside him. He put his arm around her and drew her against him. "Mmmm," he said, resting his lips against her hair. "Yes, this is it. It's exactly right, now."

She rested her head against his chest and closed her eyes. "Yes," she murmured, "it is...."

A while later, Jed stopped kissing her long enough to ask if she wanted to have dinner.

"Not really," she confessed. "I just want to sit here and kiss you."

"Thank God," he groaned. He switched off the television, which they had completely ignored for the last half hour, and drew her into his arms again. "I swear to you, Lindsey, I wouldn't have laid a finger on you if you hadn't come to me."

She smiled and nestled her head against his chest. "I know," she said. "But aren't you glad I came over?"

He reached out and toyed with a strand of her hair. "Yes," he answered at last. "I'm very glad. The big question is, are you?"

She hesitated a moment, then nodded, knowing in that instant that she had made her choice. "Yes," she said softly. "I've been fighting this a long time, but I can't fight it anymore, Jed. I don't want to fight it anymore."

"Then you forgive me for bringing you here under false pretenses?"

"Were they false?"

"No, wrong words, I guess. I only meant to have dinner with you. I wanted to see what it would be like to have you here with me, watching a Mets' game, sharing a meal, talking about inconsequential stuff like groceries and baseball and your favorite flavor of ice cream." He smoothed her hair back and searched her eyes. "What made you come sit beside me?"

"Knowing that's all it was. Realizing you were telling the truth—you didn't want to seduce me, you simply wanted my company. Knowing that made all the difference in the world. If you'd tried to smooth-talk your way into bed with me, it would have been a disaster, Jed. But you didn't. Instead, you just talked with me. That's what did it."

"And if I did want you to go to bed with me?"

She met his gaze squarely. "I'd go," she murmured.

He drew her into his arms and slowly unbuttoned her blouse. Gently, his hands cupped her breasts. "I'm not quite sure I can wait to get you upstairs to bed," he murmured.

"I'm not sure I can wait, either." She ran her hands underneath his shirt, savoring the smooth skin of his back. Her eyes closed as the warmth of his body seemed to permeate hers. "In fact," she whispered shakily, "I don't want to wait. I think I've waited long enough already."

As if sensing her real commitment, he kissed her breasts with deepening ardor. Everything lurched into slow motion. Suddenly nothing else existed. They were alone, halfway to heaven, exploring each other with wondrous delight, undressing slowly, then lying naked together, savoring the sensation of skin against skin.

She moaned as his mouth caressed her stomach, then found the junction of her legs and nuzzled her. She felt sparks explode inside her, felt her legs part as if of their own accord as he began a slow, deep exploration of her womanhood. He answered her every wish, fulfilled every fantasy, laying claim to her as no man ever had in her life.

"You're driving me mad," she whispered, lying back as he stroked her nipples with one hand and massaged her with the other.

"You've driven me mad since the first day I met you," Jed said. "It's time for you to find out what I've been wanting for so long."

She groaned as he brought her to the threshold of ecstasy. Putting her arms around his neck, she pleaded with him to make love to her. "Now," she whispered urgently. "Please."

Time skidded to a stop. They entered paradise, leaving earth far behind, climbing toward the stars on the most wonderful journey of their lives. She clung to him, feeling the golden ripples already beginning deep inside her. "Oh, Jed," she whispered brokenly, "it's so beautiful."

He carried her to Olympus, flinging her into sunshine so bright and golden that she had to cover her eyes. At the end, she cried out in rapture, then gave herself up to the exquisite pleasure that rippled through her body....

"Lindsey."

His voice brought her slowly back to reality. She opened her eyes and stared into his face, seeing him as if she had never seen him before. "What is it?" she whispered, her voice filled with wonder.

"You're beautiful."

She felt chills break out all over her skin, felt herself begin to fall into the golden light again. "Oh, Jed," she whispered, "I never knew it could be like this."

"I always knew it could be like this," he murmured.

Dizzy and whirling, she soared again, swirled and climbed and danced, all the while held safe in Jed's arms. She inhaled the delicious scent of his body, felt the scratch of his beard, the warmth of his skin, heard his deep, contented murmurs, and she felt as if she had found her home.

But how did Jed feel? As she came back down to earth, nestled against the warmth of his body, she studied the dark hairs that matted his chest and wondered if he, too, felt how special this had been. Had he experienced the deep joy of love, or had it been just another casual encounter for him? The question frightened Lindsey because she wasn't quite sure of the answer. She wanted to believe this had been special for him also, but a doubt remained. She wondered if she would ever learn to trust him. Or would she always have reservations about him and his ability to be faithful?

"Lindsey."

"Mmmm?"

"Will you stay with me tonight?"

She smiled, automatically reassured. Her questions left her. "Yes," she whispered, snuggling up to him. "I'd love to stay with you tonight."

"Will you give me another back rub?"

She laughed delightedly. "Mmm-hmm," she whispered. "If you'll give me one."

"With pleasure," he said, kissing her deeply. "With very great pleasure." He began to stroke her back, then moved his hands to her breasts. "There's a problem though," he murmured. "My brain tells me to rub your back, but my hands keep wanting to massage your breasts."

"I don't think that's a real problem," she said, her voice breathless with renewed desire.

He fingered her aroused nipples. "Mmmm," he murmured, chuckling with satisfaction. "I can see it isn't." His kisses deepened and Lindsey felt herself falling into endless, boundless space again. She was brought abruptly back to earth when the phone rang shrilly.

Jed groaned, but picked it up. "Hello."

"Jed?"

The voice was so loud that Lindsey could hear it quite clearly. She lay next to Jed, smiling with contentment, then recognition slowly broke through and she was jolted wide awake. She knew that voice.

"I can't talk right now. I'll call you back tomorrow."

"Did the information help?" the booming voice asked.

She could feel Jed stiffen. "I told you," he said. "I can't talk right now." He sat up and turned his back on Lindsey. "I'll call you tomorrow." He hung up, then sat for a moment before saying, "Business. It never stops."

Lindsey stared at Jed's broad back. There was a terrible sinking feeling in her stomach, as if she'd just stumbled on a secret she shouldn't have. "That was Lyman Cartwright, wasn't it?"

Jed stiffened, then turned and looked at her. "Yes."

"I didn't know you did business with Lyman."

"Well..." Jed seemed to debate something, then said, "It wasn't business, really."

She swallowed. "Oh? If it wasn't business, what was it?"

He hesitated, then shrugged. "Nothing."

Lindsey's heart sank. She knew a lie when she heard it. She felt sick. Slowly, she began to drag on her clothing.

"Hey," Jed said softly, reaching out and taking her hands in his. "No need to get dressed. I'll just carry you upstairs and—"

"I'm not going upstairs," she said, her voice shaking with emotion. "I'm leaving."

"A few moments ago you were going to stay with me tonight. Do you always change your mind this quickly?"

His ironic question seemed calculated to make her feel guilty. It didn't work. She knew he was lying to her. Pain swelled within her, but she managed to contain it. "What *was* the phone call about, Jed?" She waited hopefully. He could still tell her the truth. There was still time. All he had to do was admit it. She waited, feeling as if everything hinged on his answer.

Jed hesitated, then said, "It wasn't anything important, Lindsey." He drew her into his arms. "Let's not talk about it just yet."

All hope dissipated. She felt shattered. With those words, he had chosen to go on with the charade, but she knew she couldn't. She felt as if her heart were breaking, but she had to face the truth, no matter how unpalatable it was. A terrible suspicion grew in her mind like storm clouds darkening the horizon. Suddenly she couldn't think straight, she could only see the doubts, hovering over her, blotting out all light.

"What did Lyman tell you, Jed?" she asked bitterly. "That the best way to get me was to pretend all you wanted was my company? Or was it Mother who helped you realize how to act? I can just see her selling off her own daughter to the highest bidder. But tell me, Jed, did you just want this one night with me, or were you planning a lengthier affair?"

"I wasn't planning an affair at all—"

"So it was just a one-night stand you wanted," she said, feeling her hopes crumble. "Please call your driver and ask him to come for me now. Or am I being naive again? Did you really have it planned that he'd come back at midnight, or was that just added bait in the trap, so to speak?"

He ignored her question. "Your mother loves you, Lindsey. The problem with you is, you're so filled with bitterness about the past you don't even recognize the people who genuinely love you."

"I don't need a lecture from you about bitterness, Jed," she said, pulling on the rest of her clothes. "Your actions speak much louder than your words."

"Lindsey, I don't know why you're so upset—"

"That's the problem, Jed—you *don't* know why I'm so upset."

"All right," he said. "I didn't want to do it this way, but I'll tell you now—"

"No, Jed," she interrupted. "I don't want to talk with you now. I don't think I could even listen to you. I'm not thinking clearly."

He stared at her, then nodded. "All right. I won't argue with you."

She laughed derisively, hoping to hide her pain. "I didn't think you would. You got what you wanted, after all. Why gild the lily?"

"I *will* talk with you later," Jed said, ignoring her jibe. "After you've calmed down."

"Is that when you'll let the ax fall, Jed?" she asked sweetly. "Is that when you'll sit me down for a heart-to-heart talk and discuss the impossibility of our ever working together again?"

"Lindsey, you don't understand—"

"Oh, but I do!" she cried, tears beginning to glitter in her eyes. "I've understood from the very beginning, Jed. It was you who didn't understand. I knew if I got involved with you everything would be ruined. Not for you, of course, but for *me*—" She broke off, unable to articulate the pain she felt.

"I'll talk with you tomorrow. I have a press conference scheduled at ten. I'll expect you to be there."

"A press conference?" She stared at him. Ordinarily, she scheduled his press conferences and meetings. Why didn't she know about this one?

"That's right," he said. "I'll talk with you afterward."

"Please call the limo."

"Will you be at the press conference?"

She drew a deep breath. "I'll be there."

"Good," he said, sounding relieved. "Then I'll call Leo." He picked up the phone and punched out the numbers. "Leo? Could you come pick up Ms. Andrews and take her back to El Dorado? Yes, thanks. And drive behind her to see her safely home."

"There's no need for that," Lindsey said shortly.

Jed hung up. "I think there is."

"And Jed is always right, isn't he?"

He seemed about to say something, but decided against it. He began pulling on his clothes. "As I said before, I'll speak with you after the press conference in the morning."

"Was this press conference going to be a complete surprise?"

"No, I was hoping we'd get around to talking about it tonight, but things got a little out of hand. As I recall, you came and sat by me and the next thing I knew, I wasn't thinking clearly anymore."

"How convenient," she said icily. "Blame everything on me."

"I told you earlier, Lindsey—I wouldn't have laid a finger on you tonight if you hadn't completely agreed to it."

"So now you do admit you lured me here with other motives besides just supper."

He studied her quietly. "There's always hope," he said at last.

Something about his quiet answer unnerved her. Suddenly she wondered if she was right to think that Jed's talking to Lyman Cartwright had anything to do with her.

Then she knew she was right. Jed Wentworth had called Lyman Cartwright for information about her. What other motive could he have had except to get her into bed? With a sinking heart, she realized all her hard work the past few months was for nothing. Her career at Wentworth Enterprises was over. Her father's dream would come to fruition without her being there to watch. But even worse, she was losing Jed and she'd never really had him. For a few brief, golden moments, lying in his arms, she'd thought she'd had that golden ring Margaret Oliver had spoken about. She'd been wrong.

Feeling as if her heart had truly broken, she turned listlessly toward the hall. "I'll wait by the door," she said quietly.

"Lindsey..."

She didn't turn around. "Yes?"

When he didn't answer right away, she wished she had turned around so she could see his face. When he spoke, his voice was so gentle, she felt as if a huge hand had gripped her heart and crushed it completely.

"I'll speak with you tomorrow," Jed said. "After the press conference. Perhaps things will be a little more clear then."

Why did he have to sound so gentle? She closed her eyes for a moment and willed the pain to go away. "All right," she said, then she saw the lights of the limousine coming up the long driveway. Opening the door, she stepped into the night. She didn't bother to say goodbye.

Fourteen

Before dawn, Lindsey sat in her living room, her stomach tied up in knots as she pondered the destruction of everything she had worked for. She thought of Jed and felt desolation threaten to overcome her. Sometime during the night, she had realized she loved Jed. But what did she mean to him? Was she just another fling or did he truly care for her? Last night she had jumped to some hasty conclusions, but when she'd arrived home, she had begun to think more clearly. Now she was still having difficulty making decisions: could she remain at Wentworth Enterprises and work with Jed?

Groaning, she rubbed her eyes tiredly and reached for a bottle of aspirin. Taking two, she sat and speculated on her future. It would be a disaster if she stayed at Wentworth. Everyone would think she'd got her job because she was sleeping with Jed. No one would respect her. She would be gossiped about, ridiculed, whispered over and condemned.

Her credibility would drop below zero. No matter how hard she worked, she'd never be able to make people believe she had earned the promotions or the raises she received.

It was a bleak picture, but she knew it was a realistic one. She had been aware of the pitfalls of getting involved with her boss, but common sense had taken a back seat to love. Which mattered more? Her career or Jed?

She sat staring into space, weighing the choices she had made and trying to decide on her options. There really weren't any. She could stay and be a laughingstock whose career would become sidetracked and stalled, or she could leave. There was always her old job at Peabody and Company. When she had left, her boss, Peter Potter, had told her the job would be waiting for her anytime she wanted to re turn.

But what of her dream of working with Jed on the Connecticut River Project? Ever since she'd first heard of it, her only goal had been to work with Jed, to carry out her father's dream. Now her goal was lost.

"Oh, Daddy," she whispered. "I've failed, just like you."

She began to rock back and forth, her arms wrapped around herself as if to ward off blows. Misery flooded her. She, too, was cursed with the Andrews lack of ability to see things through. Though this job had meant more to her than anything else on earth, she had allowed personal pleasure to come between her and her dream.

Then she raised her head. Was that dream really so important after all? For years, she had allowed her need to vindicate her father to rule her life. Now, for the first time, she really began to question her desire to work on the Connecticut River Project. Wasn't it vindication enough of her father and his ideas that the project he'd once championed was now being put into action? Did she have to be there every step of the way? Now that the project had taken on a life of its own, perhaps she could step out of the picture.

But wouldn't that be turning her back on her father? For ten years she had remained loyal to him and his dream. She had made his dream hers. How could she let it go now, when it was just beginning to come to life?

Her heart felt heavy as she went over and over the implications of everything that had happened today. Maybe she was making mountains out of molehills. Maybe the gossip would eventually subside and people would realize that it was her ability and not her body that had gotten her the job with Jed.

She felt hope flow back inch by inch. Perhaps she didn't have to give up her father's work. Perhaps she *could* remain at Wentworth and see it through to the end. Maybe she could be one of the few women who was able to buck society's cruel mandates and work with a boss who was also her lover, without losing credibility. Anything was possible, after all. This was late-twentieth-century America, not the Dark Ages. Men and women were now working together regularly. It was inevitable that there would be office romances and boss-employee liaisons. She'd just have to learn to hold up her head and not let the sharp tongues of gossipmongers get to her.

But all that still didn't answer the essential question: what did she really *want* in her life? What was more important—fulfilling her oath to her dead father, having a successful career, or having a relationship with Jed? Were they all incompatible, or could she have everything?

She laughed cynically to herself. The women's magazines were full of stories about women who tried to have it all and ended up with ulcers, tension headaches and disgruntled families. The problem was, she needed to make a choice, she had to sort out her priorities, yet right now she felt completely incapable of doing so. She was uncertain, afraid, and confused. She needed someone to talk to.

Lindsey kneaded her temples, which throbbed from tension. She wasn't seeing things clearly, still wasn't answering the essential question: what did she *want*? It was the one question she'd never felt capable of answering. She could say what she felt she *ought* to do, what she thought others *expected* her to do, but she had never once in her life decided for herself what she *wanted* to do. She'd been too busy trying to be the perfect woman, the one who pleased everyone but herself.

She stared at the phone, then lifted the receiver and dialed. "Mother? Can I come over right now? I need to talk with you. . . ."

Lindsey walked briskly up the sidewalk toward her mother's home. It was a chilly morning, with a definite nip in the air. Autumn had finally arrived and the trees were rapidly changing color, turning from vibrant green to red, orange and gold. The sky above was deep blue and cloudless. Wood smoke from chimneys scented the air with its perfume. She was reminded of when she was growing up, before air pollution was of such concern. Then they had raked the leaves into piles and set them afire. All during the fall, the air smelled of wood smoke, cider, ripening apples and the delicious scent of pumpkin pies baking in the oven.

She found her mother seated on the glassed-in, heated breakfast porch, wearing a blue dressing gown but no makeup. Sitting down opposite her, Lindsey suddenly realized just how old her mother had grown.

"Your call surprised me this morning, Lindsey," Eliza Cartwright said, pouring coffee. "But I'm happy to see you." She handed her daughter the cup of coffee and smiled. "What can I do for you?"

Lindsey studied her mother over her coffee cup. Finally she said, "Mother, I'm involved with Jed."

"Involved?"

"I went to his house last night. Things got out of hand. I ended up sleeping with him."

"I see.... Actually, I don't see. What does that have to do with your needing to talk with me this morning? When you called you sounded so upset. I should think falling in love with a wonderful man like Jed Wentworth would make you the happiest woman on earth."

"Mother, ever since you left Daddy and me, I've had one goal—to prove that I could make it on my own. I didn't want to be like you. I didn't want to marry to achieve success. I wanted to earn it all by myself. Everything was going well, and then I read about Jed Wentworth's new project to develop the land along the river. Then I heard about the position he'd created of director of advertising and publicity for the project and I went haywire. I had to have that job. It consumed me. And despite a disastrous first interview with Jed, despite being terribly attracted to him as a man, I got the job. Well, not *that* job, but one just as good—assistant to Jed for the project."

"So you've achieved your goals," Eliza said. "I'm very proud of you, Lindsey, and you should be proud of yourself."

"But I haven't, Mother! Don't you see? I let myself get involved with Jed and now it's all a mess. No one will ever believe he hired me because I'm capable of doing a good job. They'll think he hired me because he was sleeping with me, or had it in mind. My credibility's destroyed. So, here I am, ending up exactly the way I didn't want to end up—not achieving success on my own, but the way you did it—by getting involved with a successful man."

Eliza stared into her cup, then set it down. She smoothed a hand over her dressing gown, then peered at Lindsey. "So you're saying that you haven't been able to show me up, is that it? All these years you wanted to be better than your mother and you've just realized you're exactly like me. It must be a bitter pill to swallow."

Lindsey put a hand to her forehead to shield her eyes. She couldn't stand looking at her mother, who suddenly seemed as shrewd and wise as an ancient prophet. "You're very direct, Mother," she said at last. "I hadn't thought of it exactly that way but you're right, that's how I've been feeling, at least until about an hour ago."

"What happened an hour ago?" Eliza asked gently.

Lindsey swallowed the lump that had formed in her throat. "Oh," she said shakily, "I had decided to call Peter Potter at Peabody and Company and tell him I'd like my old job back. It seemed the best solution to all this mess. He'd told me when I left that my job would be waiting for me if I ever wanted it back. But then I began to think about how I've been a damn fool these past ten years. I've devoted myself to hating you and revering Daddy. I've made a Holy Grail out of proving that I could do what you couldn't—make it on my own, without a man's help. And I could have, I suppose, if I hadn't fallen in love."

"So it's not just a fling?" Eliza asked. "You really love Jed?"

Lindsey nodded, lowering her head in shame. "All these years I hated you for what you did, when all you wanted was love. And I was too thickheaded and stubborn to understand until it happened to me."

"Falling in love does certainly complicate matters," Eliza said gently. "Life's ten times easier when you're not involved with anyone else. You can coast along and just think of yourself. When you fall in love, all of a sudden you begin to think of the other person, too." She sighed. "But I must say, I'm happy for you, Lindsey. I'd rather have a daughter who's got someone to love than a daughter who's busy climbing the corporate ladder of success."

"But that's *your* priority, Mother!"

"And it's not yours?"

"I don't know. Right now I'm so mixed up I don't know what I want—Jed or a job with Jed."

"Well, it's certainly a sticky wicket, as they say. But before I went off half-cocked, Lindsey, I'd take a while to think things through. Don't let your pride get you into a mess you don't want to be in."

"What do you mean?"

"Let's hypothesize a little, shall we? Let's say you still wanted to show me up, to prove you can make it on your own—unlike me, who, as you put it, had to marry a man to become successful. If you were feeling that way, you just might quit your job with Jed and go back to Peabody. But is that what you really want to do? What's more important to you, Lindsey? Showing me up or having someone to love? And there's another issue: your loyalty to your father. What are you going to do with your life, Lindsey? Continue living in a shrine built to your father's memory or start living for yourself for a change?"

Lindsey groaned. "Those are the exact same questions I've been asking myself for the past couple of hours."

"Then why did you come here?"

"I guess I needed to talk to you about all this, to see if maybe your priorities have been right all along, and I'm the one who's been off base."

"Lindsey, I can't be the one to make that decision. Every woman has to learn that only she can determine how she'll live her life. For years, I tried to be what others told me to be, a good wife, and for years I was miserable. And in trying to be the perfect wife that society and my parents told me I should be, I made life miserable for your father and for you, too. I finally decided life was too short to live it the way I was *supposed* to live it, or the way my mother or even my daughter *wanted* me to live it. Leaving Henry was the hardest decision I ever made, but I realized it was the right one.

It broke my heart when you sided with Henry and turned against me, but I knew I still had to do what I felt was right for me.

"But what was right for me might not be right for you. Maybe you're born to be a career woman. Maybe you don't need love the way I did. But maybe you *do*, Lindsey. Only you can decide what you want. And it's going to be the toughest decision of your life."

Lindsey stared at her mother, a final question urging itself into words. "Mother," she said slowly, "Jed called Lyman recently and asked for some kind of information about me. Do you know anything about that?"

Eliza hesitated, then sipped her coffee slowly, as if to give herself time to think. Lindsey felt her heart sink, but waited patiently. She'd try not to jump to conclusions today as she'd done last night.

At last Eliza answered: "I know that Lyman spoke with Jed," she said carefully. "Why? Haven't you spoken with Jed about it?"

"I was with Jed last night when Lyman called. For some reason, Jed acted guilty. I got suspicious and left."

"Suspicious of what?" Eliza asked gently.

Lindsey looked down. "It sounds foolish now, I suppose, but last night—" She broke off, unable to explain her suspicions to her mother.

"Yes? Last night?" her mother prodded gently.

"I'd just made love with Jed for the first time and I felt insecure, I suppose. When I heard Lyman calling asking if the information had been helpful, I jumped to the conclusion that Jed had asked Lyman something about me in order to get me into bed." She lowered her gaze even more, feeling ashamed of her suspicious nature.

Eliza laughed gently. "I can assure you, darling—a man as virile as Jed Wentworth would hardly need to call Lyman to ask for advice on getting you into bed."

"Then why would he call, Mother?"

"Why don't you ask him?" Eliza suggested gently.

"Do you know?"

Again Eliza hesitated, but sidestepped the question. "Lindsey, I think it would be best if you spoke with Jed about this."

Lindsey stared at her mother, then crumpled up her napkin and got ready to leave. If her mother wasn't talking, there was no sense in trying to pry the information out of her. "Thank you, Mother. It was kind of you to talk with me."

Eliza rose and put her arms around Lindsey. "I think it will all work out, honey," she said, patting her daughter's back. "Things do have a way of working out. Just have a little faith. Believe in Jed, and believe in yourself."

Lindsey nodded, then turned and walked away. Her heart had never felt as heavy, her hopes had never been so low.

There were a half dozen reporters from Hartford-area newspapers gathered in the conference room near Jed's office when Lindsey arrived at work. Crews from five television stations and six radio stations were also bustling around, setting up cameras and sound equipment, testing lights, laughing and drinking coffee and eating Danish pastries that Margaret Oliver had hastily assembled.

Lindsey spied Anne Rutledge, the business reporter who had broken the story about the official ground-breaking for the Connecticut River project, which was scheduled for next month.

"Hello, there," Anne said, approaching Lindsey. "Remember me?"

"How could I forget?" Lindsey asked.

Anne smiled humorlessly. "You're Jed's assistant, I hear. What's this press conference all about?"

"I don't have any idea," Lindsey admitted. "He sprung it on me, too."

"It has something to do with the Connecticut River project, I know that," Anne said, frowning. "Why's he being so damned secretive?"

Lindsey shrugged. "You're the reporter," she said lightly. "You figure it out."

"He hasn't told you anything?"

"Not one word. He just told me to be here."

Frowning even more, Anne gazed around the room. "Everyone's here. Why didn't he save whatever he's going to announce for the ground-breaking ceremony?"

"Maybe he felt it was so important that he needed to announce it sooner."

"But what could be that important?" Anne mused. "That's what I want to know."

"I guess we'll all have to wait and find out together."

"I guess so," Anne said grudgingly.

Lindsey slipped away and found Margaret Oliver hastily typing a memo. "Is that for the press conference?" Lindsey asked.

Margaret jumped a foot. "Oh, my Lord, you scared me!" she said, holding a hand over her heart. Hurriedly she ripped the page from her electronic typewriter. "As a matter of fact, it is. Jed wants it now. See you later."

Lindsey sighed as she watched Margaret hurry into Jed's office. Margaret was back to being the old battle-ax. Yesterday's intimate talk hadn't changed anything between them. Feeling at loose ends, Lindsey wandered back to the conference room and took a seat in the back row. She didn't feel like being conspicuous today and her heart wasn't in the press conference. She imagined it would be about some technical aspect of the project. Jed had been talking about hiring a new architect to design the Conference Center. He might unveil the plans today.

Not that it mattered, she thought desolately. Suddenly the River project didn't seem important at all. She was trying to figure out where she was going in her life and her old priorities were no longer the focus of her attention. Right now, she was more interested in seeing Jed. She could feel her nervousness increase as ten o'clock approached. Her heartbeat quickened and her palms grew moist. Suddenly she wanted nothing more than for this silly press conference to be over so she could talk with Jed.

At last he walked in, looking unbelievably handsome in a gray suit and a red tie. Lindsey's heart swelled as she remembered last night, then she felt regret take over. If only she hadn't been such a fool and overreacted last night. If only she hadn't jumped to conclusions about Jed.

"Thank you for coming," Jed said into the battery of microphones.

The reporters scurried to their seats, opened notepads, whispered to each other, signaled to cameramen, hurriedly finished coffee, then settled down to hear what Jed had to say.

Seated in the back row, Lindsey took an unsteady breath and willed the hands on the clock to move more quickly. She really didn't care what Jed was saying, didn't give a damn about the silly architect who was designing the Conference Center. Stifling a yawn, she wished she'd gotten some sleep last night. She glanced at her watch, looked longingly at the urn of coffee and tried to remember what she had scheduled for this afternoon. Then, slowly, Jed's words broke into her thoughts, claiming her attention. As she began to listen, she grew increasingly still. What was he saying? What was this all about?

"...and though I'm proud to be developing the land along the Connecticut River, I can't claim to be the first man who thought of the idea. Twenty years ago..."

Lindsey grew dizzy. For a moment she thought she might faint. Jed's words faded. The room grew dim. She clutched the edge of her chair and forced herself to listen.

"...this man went to all the banks, all the financial institutions, asking for backing, but he was turned down by everyone. People laughed at him—they called him a dreamer, an idealist. Some even said he was a fool...." Jed's voice trailed off. He looked over the heads of the reporters, found Lindsey, and met her rapt gaze.

"But he wasn't a fool. He was a man who lived before his time. That's been the unfortunate fate of lots of good men—they get ideas that never come to fruition. They have visions of what can be, dreams of making a better world. I think this man was like that—a dreamer, whose ideas were so big and so wonderful, that the world wasn't ready for them in his lifetime."

Lindsey felt a huge lump in her throat. Her eyes misted with tears and she had to blink them away. But her heart was soaring. She hung on Jed's every word, her eyes glowing as she listened.

"Most people thought that man was a failure," Jed continued. "He *was* a dreamer, and many people belittle that. Our society only values the doers, the achievers. The man who sits and dreams, but can't bring his dreams to life usually isn't admired."

Jed took a breath, letting his eyes sweep the conference room, which had grown unusually quiet. "I recently met someone and found myself discussing how to judge a person—by appearances, or by what they have accomplished. It was an interesting conversation, but I think perhaps both of us lost sight of something very important. Perhaps, ultimately, we can only judge others by the depth and breadth of their dreams, by what they wish for, hope for, strive to accomplish. Whether they achieve it in their lifetimes seems now not to be as important as whether they tried."

Tears shimmered in Lindsey's eyes as she listened to Jed. She didn't know where all this was leading, but she knew he was giving her a gift more precious than any words of love murmured in a moment of heated passion. Beauty reigned, and the possibilities for the future seemed suddenly limitless, where only hours ago there had seemed to be no hope at all.

Jed paused, then he spoke again: "The man I've been speaking of was a quiet man. He never was successful, as we define success so often in our society. He didn't belong to the Businessman's Club, or the Hartford Club, or any of the prestigious country clubs west of Hartford. He didn't live in a huge house or drive an expensive car. He lived simply, almost frugally, surrounded by his beloved books, with a daughter who loved him very much.

"This man's name was Henry Carter Andrews. He was, by and large, an unsuccessful real-estate developer who died eight years ago. I looked up his obituary in the paper yesterday. There were no headlines, no list of organizations he belonged to, no honorary posts held. He died unknown and has remained unknown, but today I'm announcing that this man's dream will come to fruition—the riverfront development project he believed in so much will bear his name. From here on out, the Connecticut River Project will be known as the Henry Carter Andrews Memorial Plaza." Jed nodded to the assembled reporters and stepped back. "Thank you very much."

He was gone in a shower of exploding flashbulbs. Lindsey sat and blinked, feeling dazed by all that Jed had said. At first she couldn't assimilate what had happened. It was all so completely unexpected that she felt off-kilter, as if someone had tipped over her chair and she was falling through space, disoriented. She sat and let the realization of what Jed had done sink in, and slowly she began to understand. With comprehension came a strange mixture of gratitude, awe and shame.

Now she understood. Now she saw it all clearly. The glass through which she looked was no longer cloudy, her vision no longer distorted. Her face grew hot at the memory of how she had mistrusted Jed. That phone call to Lyman Cartwright hadn't been about how to get her into bed. Instead, Jed had been probing her background, trying to find out what had motivated her to take the job with him. And when he had found out, he had done the most beautiful, loving thing he could ever do—he had given Lindsey the fulfillment of her lifelong dream; he had given her father his place in Hartford's history.

Feeling drained of all emotion, Lindsey stayed seated as the reporters and camera crews slowly filed out of the room. Anne stopped as she walked by Lindsey. "It was a nice touch," she said, "but I still can't figure out why he couldn't wait to announce this at the official ground-breaking...." She frowned thoughtfully, then shrugged. "Oh, well, go figure." Then she was gone, and Lindsey sat and stared after her.

"I bet I could tell you why," she whispered, then looked at the door to Jed's office. At least she thought she knew: he'd done it for her. He hadn't wanted to wait for another month to go by. Perhaps he had sensed that the tension that simmered between them was close to exploding. Perhaps he had sensed that Lindsey might still doubt his motives. What better way to show her he cared than dedicating his project to her father?

Humbled, she sat and stared at Jed's closed door. She had to go to him, had to find some way to thank him, to explain her mistrust of him. But she felt inadequate, badly flawed. She wondered now if he could ever love her after the way she had treated him last night. Perhaps he wouldn't want anything more to do with her. Perhaps she had failed him so miserably that he would see her for what she was—unloving, uncaring, ungiving.

Her heart wrenched with pain and she sat with bowed head and reflected on the hard lessons she was learning about herself. Self-knowledge was never an easy thing, she realized, but her own journey toward the truth seemed particularly devastating. Perhaps each and every person wanted to see only the best in themselves. Most were not prepared to face their own failings and inadequacies. But they were there, shadowing one's life like angry storm clouds.

Lindsey knew then that her greatest challenge still lay ahead, behind the closed door that led to Jed's office. She could go to him with bowed head, filled with anguish at her shortcomings, or she could go to him with a heart full of gratitude and love. She had no idea how she would respond, which way would feel right, which would be appropriate, knew only that she had to go to him.

Slowly she rose and walked toward the door. When she opened it, Jed raised his head immediately. They stared at each other, unmoving, then Lindsey broke the trance by softly closing the door. Suddenly she knew there was only one thing to do.

She approached his desk. "That was the most beautiful thing anyone has ever given me," she said softly.

"I sat there, and when I heard what you were saying, your words went into my heart and I understood, perhaps for the first time in my entire life, the true meaning of love." Her eyes were luminous, filled with love, yet tinged with sadness. "How can I ever tell you adequately what this means to me? How can I ever find the words to express my joy?"

"You just did," he said gently.

She smiled, her eyes drinking him in, feeling chills break out over her skin, feeling her heart fill up with warmth. She bowed her head. "I'm sorry," she whispered. "So very sorry."

"For what?" Jed asked tenderly.

"For the way I treated you last night."

He took a deep breath. "I think I understand what you were feeling."

Her head came up. "How can you?"

"Stop blaming yourself, Lindsey. What else could you think with the way I was acting? When Lyman called I got scared. I hadn't gotten around to telling you what I'd found out about your father and I was worried you'd be suspicious. I bungled things. Right then I should have hung up the phone and turned to you and told you everything. Instead, I tried to cover up—a fatal mistake for anyone. I tried to pretend the phone call wasn't about you, and you could tell I was lying. It was the lying you were responding to, I imagine, not so much the fact that I'd been talking to Lyman Cartwright about you."

"You understand so much."

He gazed at her with loving eyes. "I've understood something from the very beginning," he said. "From the moment you walked out of our first interview, I knew I wanted you. You were so feisty, so determined, I just wanted to scoop you up and carry you off to bed. And for a while, I thought that's all it was—just desire."

Lindsey ran her fingers over Jed's highly polished desk. "And that's not all it is?" she asked softly.

"Not anymore. Perhaps that's what it was in the beginning, and you sensed it. The more I chased, the more you ran. It was fun, but somewhere along the line, I'm not exactly sure when, it stopped being a game and became real."

"What are you saying, Jed?"

He steepled his fingers and rested his chin on them, studying her as she gazed down at his desk top.

"I love you, Lindsey," he said quietly.

Her head came up and her eyes found his. Joy expanded within her. "I love you, too."

He seemed to relax. His eyes began to twinkle. "Now I know you've got these doubts, Lindsey—"

"Doubts?"

"Doubts. You want to make it on your own. You think people would talk if they found out we were involved. So I think there's only one solution."

Her heart fell. Would he ask her to leave Wentworth Enterprises? She forced herself to swallow. "Yes?"

He shook his head and stood up and began to pace. He shoved his hands into his trouser pockets and sighed, coming to a stop in front of her. "I *think* this is the only solution, Lindsey."

She stared up at him, so anxious she couldn't see straight. "What is it?"

"We can't have people talking about us, gossiping and tittering, now can we?"

She shook her head, her eyes beginning to mist with tears. "No," she whispered. "I've never wanted that."

"Well, I don't want it, either."

She swallowed. "Of course not."

"So, as I see it, there's really only one answer."

"Yes?" She could barely stand to look at him. She didn't want to hear him tell her she'd have to leave. Though she knew she could go back to Peabody and Company, she didn't want to. Her heart was here. It would always be, for the rest of her life.

"Well," he said, reaching out and touching her hair gently, "I think we'll just have to get married." She stared up at him, afraid to believe what he'd said. He shrugged. "Of course if you see things differently we can discuss it. We *will* discuss it." He broke off and looked at her. "*Do* you see things differently?"

"Oh, Jed," she said, throwing her arms around him, laughing and crying with happiness. "No, that's exactly how I see things, too!"

Picking her up, he whirled her around joyfully. "Lindsey," he murmured, burying his lips in her hair. "Oh, Lindsey, I love you so much."

"And I love you."

"And we'll get married?"

"Yes."

"And you'll continue to work with me?"

"Yes."

"And have babies someday?"

She nodded, her eyes filled with tears of joy. "Mmmm-hmmm."

"And you'll love me forever?" he asked softly, cupping her face in his hands.

"Forever," she whispered.

As Jed drew her into his arms, she knew she had found the precious golden ring that had eluded Margaret Oliver. "I'll have to tell Margaret," she thought as Jed's lips came down toward hers. "I'll have to tell Margaret that it's worth it, that sometimes a working woman's dreams do come true. . . ."

And then her thoughts were blotted out by Jed's kisses and by the knowledge that she'd found, at long last, everything she'd searched for.

* * * * *

INDULGE A LITTLE SWEEPSTAKES

OFFICIAL RULES

SWEEPSTAKES RULES AND REGULATIONS. NO PURCHASE NECESSARY.

1. NO PURCHASE NECESSARY. To enter complete the official entry form and return with the invoice in the envelope provided. Or you may enter by printing your name, complete address and your daytime phone number on a 3 x 5 piece of paper. Include with your entry the hand printed words "Indulge A Little Sweepstakes." Mail your entry to: Indulge A Little Sweepstakes, P.O. Box 1397, Buffalo, NY 14269-1397. No mechanically reproduced entries accepted. Not responsible for late, lost, misdirected mail, or printing errors.

2. Three winners, one per month (Sept. 30, 1989, October 31, 1989 and November 30, 1989), will be selected in random drawings. All entries received prior to the drawing date will be eligible for that month's prize. This sweepstakes is under the supervision of MARDEN-KANE, INC. an independent judging organization whose decisions are final and binding. Winners will be notified by telephone and may be required to execute an affidavit of eligibility and release which must be returned within 14 days, or an alternate winner will be selected.

3. Prizes: 1st Grand Prize (1) a trip for two to Disneyworld in Orlando, Florida. Trip includes round trip air transportation, hotel accommodations for seven days and six nights, plus up to $700 expense money (ARV $3,500). 2nd Grand Prize (1) a seven-night Chandris Caribbean Cruise for two includes transportation from nearest major airport, accommodations, meals plus up to $1,000 in expense money (ARV $4,300). 3rd Grand Prize (1) a ten-day Hawaiian holiday for two includes round trip air transportation for two, hotel accommodations, sightseeing, plus up to $1,200 in spending money (ARV $7,700). All trips subject to availability and must be taken as outlined on the entry form.

4. Sweepstakes open to residents of the U.S. and Canada 18 years or older except employees and the families of Torstar Corp., its affiliates, subsidiaries and Marden-Kane, Inc. and all other agencies and persons connected with conducting this sweepstakes. All Federal, State and local laws and regulations apply. Void wherever prohibited or restricted by law. Taxes, if any are the sole responsibility of the prize winners. Canadian winners will be required to answer a skill testing question. Winners consent to the use of their name, photograph and/or likeness for publicity purposes without additional compensation.

5. For a list of prize winners, send a stamped, self-addressed envelope to Indulge A Little Sweepstakes Winners, P.O. Box 701, Sayreville, NJ 08871.

DL-SWPS

INDULGE A LITTLE SWEEPSTAKES

OFFICIAL RULES

SWEEPSTAKES RULES AND REGULATIONS. NO PURCHASE NECESSARY.

1. NO PURCHASE NECESSARY. To enter complete the official entry form and return with the invoice in the envelope provided. Or you may enter by printing your name, complete address and your daytime phone number on a 3 x 5 piece of paper. Include with your entry the hand printed words "Indulge A Little Sweepstakes." Mail your entry to: Indulge A Little Sweepstakes, P.O. Box 1397, Buffalo, NY 14269-1397. No mechanically reproduced entries accepted. Not responsible for late, lost, misdirected mail, or printing errors.

2. Three winners, one per month (Sept. 30, 1989, October 31, 1989 and November 30, 1989), will be selected in random drawings. All entries received prior to the drawing date will be eligible for that month's prize. This sweepstakes is under the supervision of MARDEN-KANE, INC. an independent judging organization whose decisions are final and binding. Winners will be notified by telephone and may be required to execute an affidavit of eligibility and release which must be returned within 14 days, or an alternate winner will be selected.

3. Prizes: 1st Grand Prize (1) a trip for two to Disneyworld in Orlando, Florida. Trip includes round trip air transportation, hotel accommodations for seven days and six nights, plus up to $700 expense money (ARV $3,500). 2nd Grand Prize (1) a seven-night Chandris Caribbean Cruise for two includes transportation from nearest major airport, accommodations, meals plus up to $1,000 in expense money (ARV $4,300). 3rd Grand Prize (1) a ten-day Hawaiian holiday for two includes round trip air transportation for two, hotel accommodations, sightseeing, plus up to $1,200 in spending money (ARV $7,700). All trips subject to availability and must be taken as outlined on the entry form.

4. Sweepstakes open to residents of the U.S. and Canada 18 years or older except employees and the families of Torstar Corp., its affiliates, subsidiaries and Marden-Kane, Inc. and all other agencies and persons connected with conducting this sweepstakes. All Federal, State and local laws and regulations apply. Void wherever prohibited or restricted by law. Taxes, if any are the sole responsibility of the prize winners. Canadian winners will be required to answer a skill testing question. Winners consent to the use of their name, photograph and/or likeness for publicity purposes without additional compensation.

5. For a list of prize winners, send a stamped, self-addressed envelope to Indulge A Little Sweepstakes Winners, P.O. Box 701, Sayreville, NJ 08871.

© 1989 HARLEQUIN ENTERPRISES LTD.

DL-SWPS

INDULGE A LITTLE—WIN A LOT!

Summer of '89 Subscribers-Only Sweepstakes

OFFICIAL ENTRY FORM

This entry must be received by: Nov. 30, 1989
This month's winner will be notified by: Dec. 7, 1989
Trip must be taken between: Jan. 7, 1990–Jan. 7, 1991

YES, I want to win the 3-Island Hawaiian vacation for two! I understand the prize includes round-trip airfare, first-class hotels, and a daily allowance as revealed on the "Wallet" scratch-off card.

Name ____________________

Address ____________________

City __________ State/Prov. ______ Zip/Postal Code ______

Daytime phone number ____________________
Area code

Return entries with invoice in envelope provided. Each book in this shipment has two entry coupons—and the more coupons you enter, the better your chances of winning!

DINDL-3

INDULGE A LITTLE—WIN A LOT!

Summer of '89 Subscribers-Only Sweepstakes

OFFICIAL ENTRY FORM

This entry must be received by: Nov. 30, 1989
This month's winner will be notified by: Dec. 7, 1989
Trip must be taken between: Jan. 7, 1990–Jan. 7, 1991

YES, I want to win the 3-Island Hawaiian vacation for two! I understand the prize includes round-trip airfare, first-class hotels, and a daily allowance as revealed on the "Wallet" scratch-off card.

Name ____________________

Address ____________________

City __________ State/Prov. ______ Zip/Postal Code ______

Daytime phone number ____________________
Area code

Return entries with invoice in envelope provided. Each book in this shipment has two entry coupons—and the more coupons you enter, the better your chances of winning!

© 1989 HARLEQUIN ENTERPRISES LTD.

DINDL-3